Diamonds are For Cocktails

A Novel

by ZARAH

SHERS OF O.G AUTHOR GENIUSES

ıblished by E&R Publishers, New York

ww.EandR.pub

Cataloging-in-Publication information is available from the Library of Congress.

Library of Congress Control Number: 2022935151

ISBN: 9781945674419 (Softcover)

ISBN: 9781945674396 (Hardcover)

First Edition

To the memory of my husband
Eugene Charles Maillard
Better days are here

PROLOGUE

It was a lifeless night. The sunless Mediterranean whispered a quiet song, while the Empyrean Heavens brimmed with stars. A silky pale moon pierced the Côte d'Azur, better known as the decadent French Riviera. Although the temperature rose to the mid-90s, the night air was cool and refreshing, at last. At this late hour, with cocktail bars closed and lovers tucked under covers, the ghosts of glitz and glamour freely strolled the promenade. Elizabeth Taylor, Richard Burton, Cary Grant, Rita Hayworth, French actress Brigitte Bardot and even Grace Kelly floated by. A cackling den of socialites tried to keep up, but they were weighed down by diamonds and jewels.

FRENCH RIVIERA

Côte d'Azur ~ Hollywood: 1997

1

Half past midnight, in an eerie clinical workspace inside an oubliette, the body of Jane Doe was laid on the ground on her back while the room temperature remained moist and cool. The serial killer of the "FBI's Most Wanted List" appeared to have struck again. With a dot of light on, the killer documented the process by clicking a few times on a vintage camera from various angles. The flashes were blinding. CLICK...CLICK...CLICK-CLICK-CLICK.

Jane Doe was an attractive petite brunette. Casually clothed, she did not look past twenty-one nor showed visible signs of a struggle. Her throat was cut from side to side, about eight inches long, and she appeared to have been dead a day earlier. The killer, outfitted in a Hazmat-like suit with rubber gloves, grabbed the victim's ankles and began to drag her entire body, hoisting it on top of an operating table. Thus began the meticulous process of body embalmment. First, the killer honed and perfected each tool and tested its sharpness. Then he outspread a packet of surgical instruments that were filled with cutters, scalpels, forceps, and retractors on top of the side table covered in white cloth. The killer then drained all the excess blood, filled up a syringe, and injected it back into the body, treating it with chemicals to forestall the body's decomposition. Moments later, the perpetrator would expertly remove thousands of minuscule veins from the victim's eyes and take each eyeball out of its socket ever so smoothly as if it had been done countless times before.

An antique amputation set was laid out next to various exotic medieval knives, battle axes, and other strange apparatus. The killer cut out body parts and began to flay her open like "Jack Rabbit" while rolling portions of her-skin back. Then the unthinkable happened as the perpetrator disemboweled the victim's anatomy one part at a time, dismembering her as though it was some kind of ritualistic move from notorious killers like Jack the Ripper.

While the cold-blooded psychopath continued to eviscerate Jane Doe's body, the spine-tingling sound of raw human flesh was captured on film—as small chunks of her meat were carved out of her bones. Minutes later, the undertaker gathered the mutilated body parts of her arms, legs, head, and torso, placing them into the deep stainless-steel sink, and washed and dried them thoroughly with a white cloth before storing them inside vintage wooden-carved trunks and relic boxes. Her internal organs were each placed in glass jars filled with ethanol liquid. Like a mystery-riddled dream thwarting us from waking up—it was a deeply disturbing scene.

* * *

A heavenly playground for jet setters and aristocrats, the French Riviera is steeped in culture and tradition. Cobblestone streets wind around a mountain of quaint golden stone homes and small churches with flower-festooned gardens. Roman aqueducts and bridges remained surprisingly intact. Globetrotters sample wines from maturing grapevines, hoping to catch a whiff of majestic chateaus from centuries past. Legendary dishes beckon, such as the signature Bouillabaisse of Marseille, a saffron-infused tomato broth stew flavored with freshly caught seafood and herbs.

The Côte d'Azur exudes style and elegance—a slice of heaven for powerful men and glamorous women who long to be seduced even to this present day. Known to awaken jaded spirits, they dazzle in stylish vacation spots imbued with timeless Belle Époque elegance. White-tie galas with trenchant mannerisms are held in elaborate ballrooms, while champagne-fueled yacht parties in sun-kissed climates are surrounded by crystalline waters. Famous painters like Claude Monet, Pierre-Auguste Renoir, Vincent van Gogh, and Henri Matisse, along with famed novelists F. Scott Fitzgerald and Earnest Hemingway, catapulted the area to prominence in the 1920s. Lavender-scented hilltop towns, unspoiled landscapes, colorful water lily ponds, glimmering beaches, seaside cafés, and sleepy fishing villages inspired their craft. At night, peninsulas like Cap d'Antibes and Saint-Jean-Cap-Ferrat capture endless stretches of glowing lights crowning atop their charming villages in one glorious, magnificent vision. A coastal town of sweeping sandy beaches, Saint-Tropez is known for its chilled rosé wines and relaxed summer parties. Sophisticated ports like Nice are calling, as is the beguiling fishing village of Villefranche-sur-Mer, all the way to the glamorous Principality of Monaco. The Côte d'Azur's extraordinary offerings give every visitor the impression of their lifetime.

French locals, by contrast, simply called it home. Their paradise resonated with fantastical events from the past, stories that literally buttered their local bread. A fisherman who lost his wife to a tragic accident restored her to life through sacrifices of human blood during the full moon. Putting a damper on tourism, the story eventually drew tourists grieving the loss of a spouse.

Over the years, stories included a dreadful tale about wild animals bellowing from being slaughtered in an abandoned farmhouse, the owner of a local winery viciously stabbed to death by his son, and heated debates over whether or not the man's organs were fed to the animals in the barn.

There were fantastical stories about a "white lady" ghost on the cliff-side and a half-human horse prancing about the village during summer nights. Stranger than fiction stories poured in by the dozens, including the true-life massacre of a wealthy aristocrat's entire family and the tantalizing fact that he took his own life soon thereafter.

* * *

On a terrace balcony perched on the edge of a precipitous cliff stood a beautiful woman donned in a v-neckline satin nightgown embroidered with Versailles French lace. Scalloped-trimmed edges caressed her porcelain skin. Dark brown hair, lifted by the wind, veiled sparkling eyes. Dainty as snow and fragile as silk cloth, she was an ethereal figure. There was a calmness about her as if a mystical apparition from the hereafter. Flashes of memories ebbed and flowed as she stared absently out to the sea. It was all she could think of.

Two weeks later, halfway across the world in Los Angeles, a determined production assistant strode across the MGM Studios to deliver the news.

"We're ready in fifteen minutes, sir," she warned.

"Fine." A renowned film director nodded inattentively as he thumbed through the final shooting script. He then bellowed to a crew inundated with far more work than they could handle for the day.

"Alright, everyone! Quiet on the set, please!" he announced sharply. "We're about ready here!"

Muttering about the months of grueling hours and fears that they would not be paid, the crew dispersed to their respective corners.

"I got a word she's arrived, and her car just entered the lot," one staff member claimed. "But that was a while ago."

"Yeah, I heard the jet didn't even get to the airport until noon," said another. "Go figure."

"And I hear this one has Estelle Bonnefontaine for talent but with the demands of Betty Davis," added a third crew in the group.

"Who the hell is Estelle Bonnefontaine?" a man asked. "Exactly the point," answered the third one.

"But is she going to be this difficult until we're done filming?" whispered someone in the back.

"I hope not," a fourth reacted.

The film was running behind schedule. The main star had been missing for days; a crew member fell off a scaffold and broke his leg, while staff rushed here and there to undo their own mistakes. Studio bigwigs, under pressure to wrap up the film, directed their ire at the first director in charge. Facing insurmountable numbers and, therefore, a huge loss of profit, the bosses were clearly not happy about moving the premiere date yet again. It was one of the worst days the production crew could recall. Everything in the plan had gone colossally wrong, and all were simply exhausted.

The film crew was by now immune to the widely-accepted trade-off, namely bragging rights to their friends and families about working in glamorous Hollywood. They were losing patience quicker than they signed up for the project they once proudly discussed. Many awaited paychecks for months. The singular word missing from the script was the only word on their minds: PAYDAY.

"Well, for heaven's sake, don't make yourselves too useful now," a glamorous lady remarked dryly.

She was wearing a tailor-made vintage Chanel couture evening gown from Paris, resplendent with real diamond studs and random patterns of tulips and daisies, hand sewn to resemble glittering stars. The designer and her team labored for nearly a thousand hours to finish the masterpiece. This high-maintenance siren, trailed by a hair and make-up entourage, gracefully strolled across the set into a lavish living room specifically built for her and thoughtfully arranged to match her personality. She lowered herself onto an opulent French tufted sofa with gold leaf trimmings, an 18th-century replica purchased by the studio just for this scene. All the while, she revealed bits and pieces of herself to the camera. A dedicated crew swarmed in, working around her in a coordinated fashion as she quietly slipped on black satin opera gloves.

Seconds later, the camera captured her elegant black birdcage veil, a glamorous hair-do and shoulders bare, along with her enviable skin at various angles—the quintessential sun-kissed skin that women longed for, incredibly soft to touch, though anyone who dared touch her without permission would lose their job.

Her bright red lips, luscious and glossy, suggested a woman of fine taste. She instructed her first assistant to fetch a bottle of her favorite mineral water—Badoit—flown in from France that morning so she could avoid dehydration. He gingerly poured the life-restoring water into a glass adorned with a gold metal straw so that her lipstick could remain intact, while another lit a cigarette drawn from a diamond-studded holder. The final touch: an exclusive selection of museum-quality diamond necklaces in a wooden jewelry chest with red velvet cloth lining—rolled out by the in-house security team.

Minutes passed. The assistant cautiously clasped her chosen diamond necklace, and the room fell silent. A bright studio spotlight highlighted her delicate neck and décolleté, framed by three-hundred-carat diamonds with a flawless teardrop in the center. She puffed her cigarette, blew a swirl of smoke, and finally yielded a bright white smile. The star was ready.

"Should we go over your lines one more time?" asked the director.

"Whatever for?" the woman said nonchalantly.

"You're absolutely right," he replied. Turning toward his crew, the director

shouted through a megaphone. "Quiet everyone on the set, please! *AND ACTION!*".

The movie clapboard snapped. The film began to roll. But Camille quickly went off script, rambling in front of the camera.

"People in the past have described me as a...scorned woman," she began. "I don't think that's accurate. In fact, I'm far from it. That's because they don't know me. Truth is, I'm just a happy girl," she continued. "I was given away when I was really young. That's when I met my James..."

Panic set in. Producers and their assistants flipped their scripts, desperately trying to find lines that matched her utterances. But the director smiled. He admired her authenticity, the raw emotion. He signaled the cameraman to keep rolling.

"He's the perfect gentleman anyone could ever wish for," she continued. "Borrowed time, like borrowed fantasies, strips away every single fiber of your being. Memories so deep, it darkens your soul to the point I can no longer breathe..."

She stared back at the camera, lost in thought. Taking a deep breath, she resumed. "I was once in a party full of strangers when someone asked me what I really thought of diamonds. At first, I laughed. Then my heart started pounding heavily, and I began to feel sensation all over my body when suddenly, I found myself drawn into the sparkling eyes of a beautiful man. 'Diamonds are for cocktails, darling,'" I replied. She then winked at the camera as quickly as it pulled back, revealing her full identity.

"Mer-ci Beaucoup! Au revoir, " she chirped in French.

"AND CUT! That's a wrap, everyone!" the director yelled out, then moved closer to his star. "That was excellent work, Ms. Rogers. I think we have what we need. And your choice of necklace was exquisite."

"Why, thank you, darling," a relieved Camille replied. "I suppose, I must have done something right, monsieur."

"You certainly did, mademoiselle," the director smiled. "I can't wait to go to post production and do the world premiere. I'm sure your mother would have been proud."

"Marvelous, darling!" she acknowledged. "And could someone please get this dreadfully heavy rock off my neck?"

"Right away, Ms. Rogers," her assistant said.

The final stages of a major motion picture that Camille Rogers executive produced in association with the MGM Studios—with a staggering hundred-million-dollar budget—was only weeks away from completion. The biopic drama was dedicated to her late mother, Claire Rogers, a diamond magnate known for her world-famous luxurious jewelry brand L'Allure, and already had Hollywood buzzing for Oscars just in time for its 100th anniversary celebration slated for the following year.

Camille's generous donations to charities for unfortunate children worldwide were highlighted at the end, along with her financial investments in a variety of award-winning Hollywood films. Camille crafted her cameo in the last scene to highlight her glamorous life with the jewelry titan—what it was like to inherit the vast fortune her mother amassed—as one of the wealthiest and recognizable faces of adopted children in the world.

The vintage couture gown she wore on set that day was created by the legendary fashion designer Gabrielle "Coco" Chanel in Paris twenty years before her death. When Camille was only five years old—mindful that Coco would not live forever—her mother requested that her close friend make her little princess a dress she could wear when she reached her late teens and beyond. For the typical viewer, the film focused on the inner workings of the diamond business. But for Camille, the film honored her commitment to Claire Rogers' lifetime achievements, her entrepreneurial spirit, and the accolades she had rightfully earned. On a deeper level, the film highlighted Claire's ability to maintain the company's success when her mother so unexpectedly passed away. By opening up about her family, Camille could provide adoring admirers, and countless consumers worldwide with a peek into their coveted lives, which had intrigued the general public for decades. It was also an opportune time to clear up petty rumors that had circled her mother for years. Glorifying Claire was Camille's proudest achievement, an expression of gratitude for her mother's unconditional love, kindness, and generosity, despite the lingering memories both women kept hidden away. Claire took her in as a baby and literally gave her the world.

She also knew it was time to rebrand her mother's diamond products for younger generations. The astonishing diamond teardrop necklace from her mother's private collection could be transformed into a global icon, a piece that young and old, royalty and the rich, would love to collect. It would gain worldwide attention like the "Hope Diamond Necklace" donated by American jeweler Harry Winston or the well-publicized Taylor-Burton Diamond dazzler put on display by famous museums. Exquisite, intriguing, and elegantly understated—it is utterly mystifying.

Every diamond has a unique story. Jewelry connoisseurs, top collectors, and owners worldwide typically investigate a diamond's origin, value, and journey, riddled at times with more mysterious questions than answers. Camille's necklace spanned many generations dating back centuries.

Reflected under a prism of light, diamonds can signify power, strength, fears, and weaknesses. In honor of Camille's adoption, Claire branded her diamonds with the purposes they served. For an average merchant, however, the higher the price, the better, as dictated by the four Cs: COLOR, CLARITY, CUT, and CARAT. For Camille, however:

The First C represented her name—CAMILLE.

The Second C referred to her—CLASS.

The Third C symbolized her—CHARACTER.

The Fourth C signified her—CHARISMA.

This was Camille Rogers' world.

CAMILLE

Monte Carlo: 1966 – 1974

2

Camille Jeanne-Marie Rogers was raised in a palace in Monaco, one of the wealthiest towns in the French Riviera. The staff included liveried servants, butlers, and an army of domiciles. Her nursery was built for a Royal Baby.

A 17th Century French Renaissance painting featuring a radiant fairytale princess wearing a sparkling diamond crown hung above the child's bed. Commissioned by her mother from a relatively unknown French artist named Michel Dubois, the painter was now celebrated by top art collectors and curators across the globe. Crystal chandeliers adorned the ceiling. Hand-made giant plush toys and elegant porcelain dolls were strategically placed around the room, with two gold leaf painted armoires and matching drawers standing side by side. A royal crib with a luxurious silk canopy draped in swags and corona silk tassel-fringes stood in the center. A "Moses basket," hand-stitched with waterfalls made out of French Chantilly lace, was close by. Gold baby rattles and a princess crown were placed atop a down-feathered minuscule pillow. The room was magical from beginning to end.

Claire ordered staff members to treat the lavish nursery as Camille's magical castle. "You are not to wake her up until the princess is ready to do so—comprenez vous?" The stern matriarch instructed in her British accent.

"Oui, madam," complied the house servants in unison.

Housemaids caring for the child's daily needs were under strict rules of engagement. Timely meals of pasteurized milk imported from Switzerland daily were to be served in warm bottles on a silver platter, supplemented by natural baby foods free of chemicals prepared in the main kitchen.

Claire would gently scoop her up from the crib, cradle her in her arms and say, "You are the diamond of my eye, my darling royal princess!" She would then give her a big fat kiss on the lips, and Camille would giggle back. Her baby babble and infectious smile captured Claire's heart.

Claire was grooming her daughter to continue her blue-blooded family business rooted in London's affluent Mayfair district in the 1800s. In her last Will and Testament, Claire established a Trust for Camille as the sole beneficiary of all her assets, with total control of L'Allure when she came of age. This plan of succession established Camille—at twenty-one—as the fifth wealthiest woman in the world by the late 1980s. Claire's fame and accolades included charitable works for children around the globe through her foundation, which Camille willingly continued.

Camille epitomized the classic story of a beautiful baby adopted by a rich woman unable to bear children of her own. However, Claire quickly learned that adopting a child was not a glamorous task. On the contrary, it was a rigorous exercise even for the powerful. Her three-year search brought her to the Children's Home Society, where movie star Joan Crawford adopted her twins and June Allyson, her daughter. Unfortunately, founder Georgia Tann snatched over five thousand babies from the streets, shanty towns and hospitals, selling them in turn to unsuspecting families. Claire claimed that she was unaware of these nefarious activities at the time. Camille's birth parents—a young American couple—sold their baby for five hundred dollars after the Society threatened to disclose the mother's use of illicit drugs. Claire permanently sealed Camille's records through the court system, which barred anyone from learning the identity of her biological parents or their background.

The child was lavished with French-laced baby clothing, along with diamond-studded dolls and expensive toys. Claire gifted presents in advance for her birthday or when there was no occasion at all. The little princess certainly did not mind. Camille had many wonderful memories of her mother during those earlier years. She recalled flying on a Lear Jet Claire purchased back in the sixties. It was the very first private jet sold, similar to the plane in Audrey Hepburn's "How to Steal a Million." Claire introduced Camille to yachting while still a toddler. She owned a fully staffed three-hundred-feet luxury yacht featuring panoramic views, floor-to-ceiling windows, two swimming pools with spacious sundecks, a helipad, and a garage. And how could she forget the time they flew to Paris for a quick Christmas shopping trip? Amazed when she first viewed the Eiffel Tower, she thought it was a gigantic Lego toy. Then there were lavish vacations in London, the Swiss Alps, and of course, Hollywood, when Claire brought her to Metro-Goldwyn-Mayer Studios, 20th Century Fox, and Warner Bros. A compassionate child who wanted to help those in need, Camille demonstrated kindness and generosity from an early age—refusing to adopt the privileged behaviors that typically characterized wealthy children. Spoiled to the core, she refused to use or abuse her power or wealth.

Camille was pleasant to be around, mindful about her manners with the staff, and generous. She secretly traded her jewels and expensive toys for money to help a worker's child remain in school or to feed a family. Mindful that she was adopted, Camille longed to exceed her mother's expectations. She was also a good judge of character with a remarkable sense of the real world.

"Oh, you should come and meet my lovely princess, darling!" Claire boasted proudly to an associate over afternoon tea at the ritzy Hôtel du Cap in Cap d'Antibes. "She is truly a gift from God!"

"How splendid, my dear!" the woman said. "If you throw one of your fabulous dinner parties, I will surely come!" she jested.

Camille was a vision of beauty, dainty and feminine, with long brown hair, tantalizing eyes, and a tiny waist. With a lovely singing voice, she often entertained family and friends. All in all, she was a happy little girl with a vivid imagination. She was also fearless and rarely cried.

James Thomas Hughes, the son of a trusted family servant, was Camille's favorite playmate and best friend. Golden blonde hair with wispy bangs covered his piercing blue eyes. Caring but strangely subdued on most occasions, he was generally known as a shy boy who avoided people when he could. At times, he appeared disinterested, aloof.

But privately, he was an engaging child—especially toward Camille—and could hold his own in all circumstances. James remained estranged from his Welsh father, who resided in the United Kingdom. Before his father left, he worked in construction. His father brought him as a toddler to the Chateau while he waited for Mrs. Hughes to finish her duties. Claire did not seem to mind. James eventually came nearly every day. The two would play games, do outdoor activities or whatever they were in the mood for. James gave Camille joy, and she looked forward to their meetings since she was otherwise surrounded by adults.

James eventually assisted his mother on household chores, earning a few Francs on the side. During his teen years, he assisted the family's head butler, Mr. Peter Thompson, whose arthritic knees often prevented him from doing strenuous activities. The grayish silver-haired British steward in his late sixties, outfitted in a crisp black-and-white tuxedo uniform with white gloves, was the quintessential servant. He ran the Rogers Chateau with precision and pride, hiring and firing the staff, and working closely with the head of house servants, Mrs. Hughes. But James had the most difficult job: making Claire's heart beat a bit faster. Every weekend, he presented Claire with a freshly-cut colorful bouquet of flowers handpicked from the garden.

"This is for you, Madam Rogers," James offered gallantly.

"Well, aren't you just a darling little boy," a very pleased Claire replied back. "Oh, I brought one for the princess, too," he smiled.

"I have no doubt, young man." Claire played along.

"Although the prince should really present it himself, don't you think?" Claire added. "She'd be very happy to see you."

James had a crush on Camille. They chased one another about the property and garden. They teased and hurled insults, but hugged a few minutes later. They even shared bath times, two peas in the pod, when they were very young. He could comfort her with merely a wink or a look.

If Camille adored James, she idolized Claire. Baking her mother a loaf of French bread, weaving a birthday basket, or reading passages of Claire's beloved Bible while her mother relaxed on a couch, she did all in her power to demonstrate fealty and love—thanking God daily for the blessings that had come her way.

By eight, Camille was raising adult topics over dinner, including epidemics plaguing children in Africa, the Pope's visit to France, and even the history of Queen Marie Antoinette and King Louis XVI of France. She also raised questions about her mother's business and the origins of the diamond mining industry. When a top jewelry magazine reporter interviewed Claire one Sunday morning, Camille soaked up Claire's answers like a thirsty sponge.

CLAIRE

Côte d'Azur ~ Monte Carlo: 1968

3

The diamond industry was booming and Claire was thriving. An increase in demand for rare-colored stones throughout Europe, the United States, Japan, and China led to skyrocketing prices. Manufactured exclusively at Eze Village in Côte d'Azur, Claire's luxury brand included high-end jewelry, fine watches, eau de parfum, make-up, and even skincare products. Claire covered all the gamut.

Claire was innovative, a forward-thinker, and ten steps ahead of her competitors. Controlling the smallest details, she demanded that her staff work harder to perfect their craft. Pressing the importance of the company's success, she insisted that a benefit to L'Allure was a benefit for all. In meetings, she offered long-winded stories about her love for the company.

"There's no business as glamorous as the diamond business," Claire shared proudly. "Remember that to your grave, everyone."

Tight-lipped and brain-weary, senior executives nodded enthusiastically when she regurgitated the same tired phrase year after year.

"And once again you are correct, Mrs. Rogers!"

"Of course, I am darling!" Claire replied with confidence. "That's why I'm the one who pays your handsome salaries," she reminded.

* * *

Claire's grandfather, a nobleman from the wealthy streets of Westminster in East London, married a French aristocrat in the mid-1800s. He started a small diamond business in Paris, which he handed down to Claire's mother. Claire's parents eventually moved the business back to London, where they were met with great success. The generational legacy was again interrupted when Claire, vacationing in the French Rivera, had an epiphany. Moving the company to the glamorous Côte d'Azur could win the hearts and minds of buyers across the globe. Decades later, manufacturing and distribution remained in Eze Village, with corporate headquarters in Monte Carlo and a marketing division in Paris.

The rumors started in the late 60s. Claire Rogers was selling stock to keep the company afloat. Debunked by her team as baseless innuendo, the heiress, they loudly whispered, was worth nine hundred million Euros, just above her equally famous competitors Cartier and Chopard. Her powerful network included royalty, nobility, dignitaries, world leaders, business magnates, and Hollywood elites.

But privately, Claire was distracted. Self-enrichment, while glorious, was also boring. Craving balance and spending more time in church, she found herself longing for the child doctors told her she could not conceive. The woman who personified perfection could neither give birth nor carry a child.

Claire's relationship with her own parents soured over the years. Daily arguments over discipline, a suitable husband, and her teenage disdain for religion—having declared herself an Atheist, as teenagers often do—catapulted the couple into an acrimonious divorce. Claire felt guilty, appropriately heartbroken, but there was little she could do. Fortunately, her parents' respective wills decreed that Claire would inherit the family business and fortune.

* * *

Discovering God and Catholicism years later, Claire vowed to be kinder to the world at large, possibly including her staff. Unfortunately, given the challenges of raising a young daughter, business obligations and daily visits to the local church, she barely had a free minute. To eliminate the 15-minute drive to the local church, Claire built a chapel in the chateau. She lined the room with costly artifacts and relics—purchased from the best auction houses of course—that could help speed her prayers to God.

One priceless treasure: a dark wooden crucifix of Jesus allegedly discovered during the Crusades by the Knights Templar, which she mounted on the center wall. At the foot of the cross: A limestone box said to contain bone fragments of an Apostle—granted, it wasn't entirely clear which of the 12 it might be—took Claire months of negotiations to acquire. A 24-carat 10-inch cross embedded with colorful gems and stones—personally blessed by Pope John Paul II—was strategically placed nearby.

As Claire confided to those who inquired and many who didn't, her friendship with the Pope dated back to his years as a Bishop, well before he emerged as one of the most revered popes in the history of the Catholic Church. Corresponding over the years, the two often met in person, and he even invited her to attend secret events inside the Vatican. Their friendship, she said, strengthened her faith in and commitment to God and would no doubt be doubly rewarded when, not if, Pope John Paul II was canonized as a Saint.

* * *

One fine Sunday, the staff were busy preparing the family brunch on a grand outdoor terrace with a breathtaking view of the peaceful Mediterranean Sea. The morning mist, crisp and invigorating, carried scents of flowers from the garden below. Both locals and tourists had long considered the Rogers Chateau Estate the mini-Versailles of Monte Carlo. With masterfully painted wall murals, ornate paneling, period moldings, and high decorated ceilings, the chateau contained: fourteen bedrooms in the main house; a separate guesthouse with an additional eight bedrooms: two grand master ballrooms (on different floors); four dining rooms; five terraces (including bedroom balconies upstairs); three opulent living rooms; tennis courts and swimming pools (both indoors and outdoors); a gym and sauna; entertainment rooms, two gourmet kitchens, a wooden carved home library; and a subterranean garage filled with exotic cars, luxury sedans, and limousines.

Magnificent sculptures and works of art were on display throughout the chateau. A black and gold ornate staircase ascended from the marbled foyer to the second-floor balcony—a large elaborate French crystal teardrop chandelier lighting the way. The stately entrance featured a sculpture water fountain carved with mythological characters. A massive black iron gate inscribed with a gold leaf initial "R" led to a circular driveway surrounded by the tall hedges.

Butlers in white gloves and liveried servants in black-and-white uniforms were once again on schedule to deliver the Sunday feast, while gardeners pruned trees and nurtured the plants and flowers below. Staff members prepared an impeccably arranged table in a coordinated fashion. One group was in charge of placing the gold-accentuated dishware, another the ornate flatware and gold-rimmed glassware, while a third was charged with handling the fine linen napkins and beautiful flower arrangements.

Junior butlers opened expensive wines and champagnes, placing them in elegant ice buckets that also contained freshly squeezed juices. Mr. Thompson made three rounds of inspection to ensure that the placement of silver, plates, and glassware met Claire's high standards. The spectacular French brunch—a meal for the gods—included copious amounts of: freshly-baked croissants, French breads, European cheeses, homemade churned butter and fruit jams, succulent fruits and juices, a variety of French pastries, and peach cocktails, all made with local ingredients. Warm plates featured roast chicken stuffed with lobster and drizzled with Béchamel sauce, pan-fried Sole à la Meunière, roast beef, honey-cured ham, and French toast.

Seated comfortably swathed in his velvet robe was Claire's husband and Camille's father, Jacques Phillip Martin, debonair and handsome, with a chiseled face and charming personality. He was also an aspiring actor.

"Good morning, sir," greeted Mr. Thompson. "Would you like to have your coffee now?"

"Morning, Mr. Thompson!" Jacques replied. "Yes, don't mind if I do. It is a great day, isn't it?"

"Indeed, sir," admitted Mr. Thompson. "Springtime is quite glorious around here. I suppose you'd like your morning paper as well?"

"I would, thank you."

Mr. Thompson returned with the paper minutes later.

"Did you sleep well, sir?" he asked, handing him the paper.

Jacques flipped through his paper and replied. "Sufficient enough, I guess. Although with a life like this, it's hard to complain," smiled Jacques. "Precisely, sir. Well, if there's anything else..."

"No, I'm fine. You can go now."

Jacques relished the exhilarating early breezes of a new day. Standoffish, impulsive and spoiled, he projected a sense of entitlement, having squandered his family inheritance on women, booze, and bad investments. But Jacques played the role of Claire's loving husband to exquisite perfection, treating Camille like his own daughter. Even the staff thought he was praiseworthy on occasion.

Jacques was in a jubilant mood. Compared to his former work—swindling the wealthy for a living—he was now financially secure. He was a changed man, or so he convinced himself, notably the object of Claire's frigid heart. Sipping his coffee, Jacques soaked up the calming oasis. Claire soon joined him, trailed by a slightly nauseating perfume, but Jacques wouldn't say a word. Bearing a remarkable resemblance to Katharine Hepburn, Claire could be overbearing, but she knew what she wanted in life. Namely him.

"Good morning, sweetheart," greeted Jacques.

"You're up early. What's gotten into you?" Claire commented dryly as she beckoned to a servant to pour her tea.

"Nothing more than the usual Claire," he flashed a smile at her, then returned to his reading. "Just a beautiful morning, dear," he added.

"My, my, aren't we in a good mood?"

Claire paid little attention to her husband or their marriage, but neither cared enough to broach the subject. Jacques was too feckless to care, and Claire was too productive to start a fight. She met—or "discovered"—Jacques a few months after adopting Camille. Another epiphany! Jacques would be the perfect father figure for Camille, as well as a handsome companion when she needed one. The relationship worked to their mutual benefit.

"Mrs. Hughes, I'm ready for my eggs and Beluga caviar now," Claire instructed with a stern voice.

"Good morning, madam, sir," Mrs. Hughes responded. "Of course. Right away, madam."

"By the way, did anyone call Mrs. Rose in Beverly Hills to ensure that she prepares the house for my arrival this summer?"

"I was going to do it today..." Mrs. Hughes hesitated.

"I see," Claire said. "Oh, one more thing, Mrs. Hughes." "Yes, madam?"

"Make sure the little one comes down soon."

"Right away, Madam." Mrs. Hughes then exited the terrace.

"Is the little princess just waking up?" Jacques asked.

"It's Sunday morning, Jacques. What do you expect?" answered Claire. Claire planned to give Camille the birthday celebration of her young life when she turned five. This elaborate fête quickly became the highly anticipated event at the Rogers Chateau. Claire wanted all details in place before leaving for her next board meeting in Los Angeles in two weeks.

"So, Jacques," she began. "Have you given much thought to my upcoming board meeting?"

Jacques paused for a moment and said, "Geez, I'm sorry, Claire. I've honestly forgotten about it." He then added. "Where is it anyway?"

"The usual. The main office where we had it last time," she responded. "I gather you know where we'll be staying?"

"The house in Beverly Hills," he answered. "Nah, I better pass. I have a script to read this weekend. And if those guys aren't happy about my performance Claire, then I'm out."

Claire seemed surprised. "But darling, I don't know why you even bother," she reasoned. "You do realize that I'm the owner of L'Allure, right?"

"Of course, dear," he smiled faintly. "How can I forget?"

"Excellent," she continued. "Listen, darling, Richard Burton and Liz Taylor know how dreadful Hollywood can be. They owe me a lot. So, if I have to get one of my studio friends to take care of your problems..."

"Except we need to move to Los Angeles if I have any hope of succeeding in Hollywood," Jacques cut in. "I really don't have enough work around here," he fretted. "I mean, some stupid modeling commercial jobs are not the same, you know. This town's dead."

Claire had promised Jacques she would move the family to Hollywood six months out of the year so he could work on his dwindling career. The part-time relocation might give him both the luck and exposure to studio heads he sorely needed in the competitive Hollywood arena. She could care less about his success, but she did hope to reduce his unpredictable spirals into depression. She also promised Jacques that he could manage some of her multi-million-dollar real estate properties in New York and Beverly Hills. But as time wore on, that plan faded. But Jacques never complained about her broken promises. The last thing he wanted was to drive her away. Claire collected many beautiful things in her life, and, for better or worse, Jacques was her best purchase.

She did not invite him to serious meetings with important friends, but she was happy to take care of him. Claire was confident that Jacques was more than satisfied with his life.

As long as she provided him with a generous allowance for his excessive lifestyle and spending habits, she could keep him on a tight leash.

"Oh darling, you're being such a baby," Claire insisted. "I tell you what, this movie business is starting to bore the bloody hell out of me."

Jacques let out a sigh and said, "I don't know. We'll just have to see, Claire."

"Well, what do you want, Jacques?" she said sharply. "Make up your mind, darling. One way or another."

Minutes later, Mrs. Hughes walked in holding the adorable five-year-old Camille's hand, then placed her between the couple.

"Well, good morning, my sweet darling!" Claire fervently greeted her. "Have you said your prayers to Jesus this morning?"

"Good morning, mummy, I did," Camille replied bashfully.

"Morning, my sweetheart!" Jacques added. "How's my little angel?"

But Camille ignored him as she took a bite of her princess-shaped French toast topped with roasted peach and doused in warm homemade maple syrup.

"So, Camille darling, I was thinking..." Claire hinted. "Why don't you and I go down to the Èze Village next weekend for your birthday? We can visit mummy's diamond and perfume factories," she revealed.

Camille lit up.

"What kind of surprise is that?" Jacques said.

"Do you see me talking to you, Jack?" Claire snapped.

Camille said excitedly, "You mean to your diamond house, mummy? The one close to where Princess lives at...Le-Le-Le Palais?" she said fractionally.

Claire looked to Jacques and smiled. "She means Princess Grace Kelly." She then turned back to Camille and said, "Yes, darling, right near where your godmother lives—Princess Grace."

"I know what she meant!" An irascible Jacques exclaimed. "I'm part French, you know."

"I know, darling," Claire said. "But I had no way of explaining it to the child." She then returned to Camille.

"Well, maybe I'll join you two for the big celebration," he smiled. Camille gave her mother a disapproving look.

"Nice try, Jacques, but you're not invited," Claire said. "It's mother-and-daughter time, remember? We'll have our family dinner when we get back, alright?" She quickly glanced at Camille and asked. "So, how about it, darling? You don't want Jacques to come, right?"

Camille slowly put her head down. Jacques then placed his hand over hers, attempting to comfort her.

"NO, NO, NO, NO, NO!" she screamed, storming back inside the house.

The bewildering display of emotions caught everyone by surprise, especially her mother. "Well, that was strange..." Claire said to Jacques, then brooded in silence.

Camille darted across the hallway, which seemed like an endless stretch of time. She then passed six-year-old James, who was listening to all the commotion hidden behind a French armoire. Outfitted in his Sherlock Holmes trench coat with a black hat, he was pretending to be the film noir detective he had loved ever since he was four. The two immediately locked eyes. Although desperate to do so, teary-eyed Camille did not utter a word. Instead, she ran upstairs. But James knew Camille all too well. He was nearly able to read her mind.

JACQUES

Côte d'Azur ~ Monte Carlo: 1971

4

Jacques understood his role as Camille's father. He represented the stability that Claire's elusive wealthy companions could not provide. Claire wanted a father figure for her daughter. Unlike past lovers, Jacques was kind and loving to her and to Camille. He seemed to love children. Jacques quickly discovered that being married to Claire was not easy. But he embraced his new role.

Few predicted that the marriage would last for more than a few months. Even when she downplayed his significance in the first year of their marriage, Jacques knew he had won Claire over, along with her trusted, loyal staff. He provided the support she needed and tried to be the best father to Camille. He understood that children must have proper guidance. He promised himself that he would see it through. His uncanny ability to bring out the best in people impressed Claire and, eventually, her closest circle. His toned body and electrifying green eyes didn't hurt. Jacques was not a hard product to sell for anyone interested to purchase.

Twenty-five years his senior, Jacques first met Claire at the famous "Festival de Cannes" in Nice two and a half years prior, introduced by a common friend. Like many aspiring actors, he wanted to be the next James Dean. Chasing one V.I.P. party after another around the world, Jacques would wander pointlessly for years in the hopes of landing a part in a major film. Claire had a number of leading Hollywood producers and directors on speed dial. Jacques was hardly blind to the opportunity when it presented itself. "He could care less because he loved her," he told his friends. It was not long before the two began a whirlwind romance, escaping to Greece, long summer nights in Paris, vacationing in London, and observed together in just about every high-society function.

"So, how's our gorgeous man?" one close friend asked Claire at a formal event. "Oh, fine darling," answered Claire with a glowing face. "Everything is just peachy between us."

Jacques was cruising the room when he locked eyes with Claire and flashed a loving smile.

"I can see that," a girlfriend sighed. "That is what I call heaven, my dear," commented another.

"Darling, I'd praise the Lord nightly if Jacques was waiting in my bed!" a third added.

"And yet you never visit a church." Claire remarked. Her friends had a good laugh.

* * *

Despite appearing in a string of low-budget movies and steady modeling contracts, Jacques longed to find a decent role. Unfortunately, Hollywood had grown weary of his familiar "old news" face.

Jacques took to family life, ingratiating himself with both Claire and Camille whenever needed. He prided himself as the family peacemaker, problem solver, and often the family therapist. He was the only person who could broker a truce between mother and daughter when strife broke out between them—thereby cementing his role as the one person they could both depend on.

Claire was determined that Camille would carry the torch and keep her legacy alive. But constant business pressures while raising her daughter soon weighed on her marriage—a hefty price she was willing to pay in order to maintain her empire. Other than keeping their daughter away from the press, the couple disagreed on nearly every major issue.

At the same time, Claire cleverly crafted an image of Camille in the public eye. Branding her as a "Royal Princess" from the outset, she told the press that "the Rogers' bloodline ran through her daughter's veins." Camille's adoption was rarely discussed at home, and Claire permitted few into her inner circle, lest they discover the truth. Jacques fully embraced the lie. Camille soon became an enigma; her life shrouded in mystery.

MRS. HUGHES

Côte d'Azur: 1967 – 1974

5

"She doesn't like to talk about it," Mrs. Hughes said one night as she led Camille to her bedroom. Camille wanted to know more where she "came" from.

"But why?" the five-year-old asked innocently.

"Because that's how your mother wants it," she tried to satisfy her. "It's just the way it is, Cami dear. Nothing more to discuss," she added.

"It's a se-cret, Mrs. Hughes...shhh!" Camille teased, placing her one finger over her lips, then flashed her an adorable smile.

Mrs. Hughes chuckled lightly. "That's right. It's one big secret love," she replied. Then in her mid-fifties, Mrs. Hughes had a profound influence on Camille. Stocky and mild-mannered, the French-Russian surrogate with dark hair and a kind face was a trusted, loyal servant. She was also mother to Camille's best friend, James.

Mrs. Hughes fled to France from communist Russia to improve her life. She refused to become just another statistic, withering away in Russia's economic collapse. Finding work in the tiny village of Eze, she met her husband, James Hughes, Sr., a year later. A good-looking construction worker originally from Wales, he controlled the family with an iron hand. In her younger years, Mrs. Hughes toiled away as a bathroom attendant, cook, nanny, and housekeeper until a wealthy owner recommended her to Claire. She took a position as one of Claire's housekeepers shortly after her son was born. The diamond tycoon promoted her to primary housekeeper after her son James began to show up at the end of her shift. Claire thought he was a delightful boy and a safe companion for Camille.

As the years went by, Camille and James grew closer. Born a day apart in February, they were baptized in the same Roman Catholic Church in Monaco—the Cathédrale Notre-Dame-Immaculée, where Camille's godmother Princess Grace Kelly married her husband, Prince Rainer III. The brown-haired, hazel-eyed girl and blonde, blue-eyed boy were a strikingly beautiful, inseparable pair. And no matter what trouble Camille might have, James always came to her rescue. He was such a good-hearted, gentle soul that Claire increased his play day visits to three a week.

Mrs. Hughes provided the support Camille needed during Claire's absences. She loved, protected, and nurtured her. Treating Camille like a daughter, she taught her many worthwhile lessons. "Never give up." "View the world in a positive light." An exceptionally caring woman, Mrs. Hughes had Camille's best interests at heart.

But recently, she noticed a change in Camille's behavior. At first, she presumed that Camille was going through a rebellious stage that could vanish as quickly as it arrived. But to everyone's surprise, Camille would increasingly act up in front of the family or find ways to create problems that baffled everyone. She was openly defiant, and no one could control her.

* * *

Two weeks prior, after a wonderful dinner, dessert, and tea, all were ready to settle in for the night. Jacques and Claire, leaning against the headboard inside the master bedroom suite, were both engrossed in works of fiction. Adorned with valuable art and exotic trimmings—cigarette cases and jewelry boxes atop a glamorous vanity dresser—the boudoir fed Claire's ego. Claire's closest friends found her exorbitant decor a bit over the top, but she disagreed. And since Claire was richer than all combined, she easily dismissed their disdain.

Claire reached for the highest standards and excess that money could buy. Mrs. Hughes understood that her boss had a massive appetite, not just for material things but for winning at all costs. Deeply competitive, Claire had mastered the art of dealing. The greater the challenge when acquiring a collectible object, the tougher she became in closing the deal. As a result, she paid the price she desired, which brought tremendous satisfaction.

As Claire's vision blurred from fatigue, she put her book down, took off her glasses, and rubbed her eyes. She then turned off her bedside lamp.

"I'm going to sleep, darling," she yawned. "I'm so busy with the company lately...I can't believe I'm so tired these days," her voice fluttered and faded.

"OK, Claire," Jacques said as he kissed her on the cheek. "Good night then." He added, "I'll be downstairs reading if you need me. I'll get a glass of milk, scoop out some cookies, and maybe even say goodnight to our little princess."

"Alright, dear," she replied softly. "But don't stay up too late, OK? I have a few things to cover with you first thing in the morning."

"Yes, I know." He answered. "Don't worry; I won't."

At half past midnight, Jacques left the bedroom, walked gingerly down the hallway, and stopped in front of Camille's door, which was always left ajar. He was vacillating whether or not to enter, in case she had already fallen asleep, but continued downstairs to the kitchen, where he poured a glass of milk and grabbed a homemade chocolate chip cookie. He then entered a decent-sized office, placing the items on top of his desk. He began to read his part in a movie script that he was auditioning for in the coming week. Halfway through the screenplay, Jacques became restless. He walked back upstairs and decided to say good night to Camille after all. He slowly cracked her door open, annoyed that Mr. Thompson had forgotten to grease the hinges. The "creaking" sound frightened Camille. As she lay to her side facing the wall, a shadow emerged. Jacques stood by the door, silhouetted against the light.

"Hello, sweetheart." he greeted in a gravel voice. "I just want to kiss my little angel good night. Is that ok?"

Camille giggled upon realizing that it was only Jacques.

"Oui papa," she smiled, turning around.

Ever since Jacques married Claire, Camille believed that he was there to care for her. And she was right. He doted on her, loved and protected her as any loving father would. Jacques frequented her bedroom to say goodnight or to read her bedtime stories. He played a critical role, but even more so given Claire's frequent absences and her constant undermining of his parenting style. Camille adored him.

"I've missed you so much..." he continued softly as he moved closer to her.

Jacques lay beside her, kissed her forehead, and rambled on about his feelings. But Camille instinctively knew that he was different this time. She felt his warm right hand touch her private parts under her silk nightdress. He then took her small cold right hand and placed it on his. Camille froze. She pressed her plush bunny toy with her other hand against her chest as she closed her eyes, unable to breathe. Numbed with fear, the palms of her hands sweated profusely. She could hear her mother's favorite commandment: You must love thy mother and thy father. Refusing her father was not an option. Camille gave in to Jacques' demands even though it felt horribly wrong. She then saw a velvety, creamy liquid on her blanket as Jacques departed the room minutes later.

It was the longest night in Camille's life. The Royal Princess, who once lived in a fantastical land, had her innocence stolen away from her. She would never be the same.

CLAIRE AND CAMILLE

Côte d'Azur ~ Monte Carlo: 1971

6

The French Riviera was framed by glorious weather that Saturday afternoon, and Camille's lavish birthday party celebration would soon begin. Guests were arriving, and the balloons and five-tier cake with a princess standing atop her castle were in place, along with more surprises for the day. Claire's good friend and Camille's godfather Chef Paul Bocuse, a much-celebrated French chef, based in Lyon, designed the cake. It was a perfect morning to tour the diamond factory, as Claire had promised.

Mr. Thompson, also the family chauffeur, stood next to a gleaming black limousine, a 1938 Bentley Sports Saloon, parked in the circular driveway. A custom-made decorative fountain sculpture imported from Italy stood in the center of the driveway. Delicately depicting a cherubic boy and girl at play, Claire believed she was graced by God when she adopted Camille. And to her delight, a 'bonus gift from God' soon appeared—Camille's de facto brother.

Dolled up in her pink tulle dress, Camille waited inside the limousine for several minutes but quickly grew impatient. She thought about the possibility of a light shower, as was often the case in mid-summer Monaco, and was afraid it might ruin her beautiful outfit. Opening the car door, she let herself out. "Mrs. Hughes! Please don't forget to bring my umbrella!" she shouted. "I want to see the boats even if it rains today. And hurry up!" Claire, looking very classy, opened the front door.

"Darling, do mind when you talk, my dear," she commented softly. "A young lady should choose her words carefully, especially when speaking to grown-ups like Mrs. Hughes."

"Yes, mummy," Camille acknowledged respectfully. "I will next time, mummy." She then turned around and shouted again. "I'm serious, Mrs. Hughes! You have to come out NOW! We're so late!"

Claire shook her head, watching the little girl. Mrs. Hughes then appeared, holding Camille's elegant pink umbrella.

"Here you go, love," she said warmly, handing the umbrella to her. "You should be prepared for your birthday tour, my little princess."

"How kind of you, Mrs. Hughes!" She lit up. "Merci Beaucoup! Thank you so much!"

Mrs. Hughes bent over and gave her a big hug. "Happy birthday, young lady!" she greeted with a smile. "How old are you now? Well, let's see..." Mrs. Hughes pondered for a second. "Perhaps I'm guessing about fifteen, wouldn't you say?" she teased. "That's it! Fifteen, right, my sweet girl?"

"NOOOO! Mrs. Hughes! I'm only five!" Camille insisted. Amused, Mrs. Hughes and Claire smiled. Both mother and daughter climbed inside the luxurious car. Driving down to the lush winding road of Côte d'Azur, Camille inhaled the panoramic view. She was euphoric since her mother's announcement last weekend about a private tour of her mother's precious diamond factory. Sticking her head out of the car window, feeling the cool French Riviera breeze on her face, she didn't have a care in the world. The little princess was happy and felt nothing but pure gratitude. She was thankful to be loved by the greatest mother in the whole world; and humbled that she, of all children, was chosen to live this incredible life.

Twenty-five minutes later, they reached Claire's diamond factory, a one-stop shop that included a manufacturing, distribution, and in-house retail store. Behind the edifice stood Claire's famous perfume laboratory. Mr. Thompson parked the limousine, opening doors for both mother and daughter. Upon entering the lobby, Claire and Camille were welcomed by a beehive of staff.

"Bon Anniversaire, Camille! HAPPY BIRTHDAY!" all greeted fervently in unison, some in French and others in English.

Startled, Camille quickly grabbed her mother's skirt hiding behind her as she pressed her body against her leg.

"Bonjour Madame Rogers; comment ça va?" greeted Claire's General Manager, asking how she was.

"Bonjour, mes bons employés. My little princess and I are fine. Merci," Claire replied. "I would like to thank you all for this very lovely birthday tour for my daughter!" An employee in the crowd then asked Camille how she was. "Bonjour jolie, dame comment allez-vous aujourd'hui?" Camille hesitated at first.

"Go ahead, darling!" encouraged Claire. "Tell them how wonderful you are!" She then turned back to the staff and added. "She's always shy around strangers but not at home. I don't know why."

"I'm, Je-Je vais bien...merci. Je suis ravi de mon anniversaire aujourd'hui mademoiselle," spoke the well-mannered five-year-old, saying she was fine and that she was excited about her birthday.

The lobby was silent. All were surprised that she spoke French so fluently at an early stage. Having secretly learned the language, Camille's accent, cadence, and intonation were better than some of Claire's employees. Camille was indeed an intelligent child. Mastering the language at the tender age of five was quite an achievement, surrounded as she was by people who spoke English. But it was just one of Camille's many gifts.

"Oh, my pumpkin!" an astounded Claire said, deeply touched. "How in the world..." she wondered, then decided to clap her hands instead. "That was fabulous, darling!" Claire added.

Camille soaked up the praise. Moments later, the two began the first part of their highly-anticipated birthday tour. They walked the hallway and saw the different stages of diamond production. Through a continuous stretch of glass window, they viewed employees in white laboratory jackets perfecting the product. Camille watched them sort through rough diamonds in various colors to determine their value. She visited the cutting center and viewed the final polishing stage, where the diamonds were transformed into sparkling jewels in silver or gold settings by a master jewelry designer. She even toured the shipping room, where Claire's diamonds were distributed to retail stores worldwide.

Mesmerized by the magical shapes, sizes, grades, and cuts, the precious gems put her in a hypnotic trance. A blue diamond shifted from emerald in the light to ruby red in the darkness. In the corner of her eye, a pink diamond, one of the rarest stones in the world, radiated in a crystal case before her eyes. She recognized instantly that this stone was rumored to have inspired the *Pink Panther* film. Cleopatra's favorite emerald, a gem of fascination for thousands of years, was only inches away. A yellow diamond designed by one of Claire's top competitors—Chopard—was said to bring happiness and prosperity. An incredibly rare red diamond was estimated at over a million dollars per carat which seemed meaningless in comparison to the weight of it's beauty in this moment.

But the most noteworthy of all, signifying love, commitment, and romance—and her personal favorite—was a diamond that her mother simply referred to as "*The Diamond*." Camille would often compare precious gems to real people, conferring personalities, depending mainly on their beauty and value. It was clear that the young girl was thrilled by the intriguing world of diamonds. Thus marked the beginning of her life-long obsession.

Claire and Camille proceeded to the perfume factory next door for a private lesson on the blending of personal perfumes. Producing one of the finest fragrances in the world, the laboratory was a division of Claire's holding company. A female employee hand-picked by Claire led the tour.

Employees wearing pink laboratory jackets filled empty bottles, which were then placed on assembly lines for a thorough inspection and finally sent to the packaging department. Wrapped in designer packaging, the perfumes were ready to be shipped out in bulk. A perfume "professor" then escorted Claire and Camille into a clinical-looking classroom where two armchair desks awaited them—with writing pads, sharpened pencils, and a few empty bottles on the side. Seconds later, Camille began a course on the origins and history of perfume, as well as tricks of the trade on blending ingredients tailored to personal taste.

"This smells like our rose garden, mummy!" A vigorous youngster said aloud. "That's right, darling!" Claire smiled. "Like our Rose Garden at home. I'm so glad you're enjoying yourself!"

Camille named her bottle "Jardin d' Eden" in French, which meant the "Garden of Eden" because the scent reminded her of her Eden-like Chateau. Minutes passed; they finished their lesson and exited through a door that led to the main lobby. Visitors were typically taken to the famous gift shop following a tour. Claire created the gift shop to boost annual sales. Her best-seller: a perfume infused with microscopic diamond particles and twenty-four karat gold shavings inside the bottle.

Camille pointed to items that pleased her while her mother watched in delight. Moments later, the birthday girl walked through the lobby with an attendant in uniform following close behind, laden with elegantly wrapped gifts. Camille "bought" presents for James for his birthday and each member of the Rogers household to show her appreciation for their work. It was a typical act of kindness on Camille's part. Family first meant James, Mrs. Hughes, and Mr. Thompson, along with her parents. Claire had steeped her daughter in diamond lessons of a lifetime in a single day.

The celebration blossomed further when Claire decided at the last minute to introduce Camille to a dear friend who, she explained, could not make it to the birthday gathering. The woman resided in a lavish 13th-century medieval fortress that towered over a majestic port below. She was a classic beauty. With an endearing personality and graceful aura, she was also a kind and gentle soul. Camille felt an instant connection as if they were kindred spirits. The two remained friends throughout Camille's teenage years. The woman was Princess Grace Kelly, and her husband was Prince Rainer III, the reigning monarch of the Principality of Monaco.

* * *

At three o'clock in the afternoon, the sun was still warm and shining. The birthday celebration took place on Claire's luxury yacht, berthed among a virtual sea of vessels belonging to the richest individuals in the world. Claire organized a variety of programs for Camille's 5th birthday, including clowns, mimes, musicians, dancers, face painters, as well as popcorn and balloon vendors.

One of Claire's many surprises was a multiracial group of orphan children tasked to sing "Happy Birthday," a once-in-a-lifetime opportunity for these impoverished children to experience wealth and abundance first-hand, if only for a day. More to the point, the invitation underscored Claire's benevolence—just how kind she could be to the less fortunate. Their presence would help Camille appreciate her life of luxury and future inheritance as a recipient of song versus singing for her supper.

While elegant hors d'oeuvres and cocktails were passed about, Claire and Camille moved to the upper deck for a private mother-and-daughter lunch, surrounded by an extraordinary view of the turquoise waters. They soon rejoined their guests to ensure that all were enjoying the party. When Claire announced the next program, children rushed to line up for her surprise. Claire and Camille gave away elegant pink gift bags with gold foil print that read, "A Gift of Love." The elegant bag included a hundred-euro bill hidden inside a porcelain princess statuette modeled after young Camille. The children could then use the figurine as their own "piggy bank."

As the sun set, the temperature cooled. Children gathered around the birthday girl huddling under pink cashmere blankets with a glittering princess imprint. Mr. Thompson and his footmen brought out hot coco served in translucent pink princess mugs painted with flecks of white reminiscent of diamond fireflies at night. Claire topped the celebration with a well-produced splendid fireworks show in the harbor, accompanied by the "happy birthday" song played in graceful orchestral music. Camille was blissfully happy, certain that she was the luckiest child to walk the earth. She could not ask for a better birthday. It was magical. It was entertaining. It was pure heaven.

JAMES

Monte Carlo: 1971

7

James was a peculiar child, a loner but seemingly with a heart of gold. Adults often commented that his quiet demeanor suggested an old soul. A distinctly attractive child, he was also extremely shy. Yet he leaped to Camille's defense whenever needed. Claire, Jacques, and the family servants treated him with respect. Camille was offended by his teasing at times but fully embraced their "brother and sister" relationship. James was her best friend and sole confidant. She repeatedly assured him that no one could ever come between them. The two saw eye-to-eye.

* * *

One lovely afternoon a few days later, Claire was sipping her afternoon tea in the family living room while listening to classical masterpieces from Mozart, Beethoven, Bach, and Chopin. The opulent room with high ceilings, expensive tapestries, and famous wall paintings suggested nobility and aristocracy.

Mrs. Hughes, gloomy with swollen eyes, quietly entered the room carrying dainty tea sandwiches with thinly sliced cucumber and smoked salmon, freshly baked scones with clotted cream and preserves, and an assortment of sweets on an elegant three-tier silver tray. Claire immediately took notice of her melancholy.

"No, Mr. Thompson today, I suppose?" she asked with an impassive tone. "Good afternoon, madam," she replied absently. "No, I'm afraid not.

Mr. Thompson caught the flu last night. I recommended he take the day off to avoid contaminating the family and staff." She then added. "Is there anything else, madam?"

"No, Mrs. Hughes. That'll be all," Claire replied, then returned to her reading. Mrs. Hughes slowly turned toward the entrance.

"Wait! That's not all," Claire insisted, placing down her book. "Do you mind telling me what in God's green earth is going on? Come on, let's hear it."

Mrs. Hughes hesitated, then hit a breaking point.

"It's just that my husband..." she began to sob. "He had a heart attack last night and died," she revealed.

Mrs. Hughes was devastated to learn that Mr. Hughes had passed away without warning. She stayed up all night long worrying about her children and their future.

"Well, isn't that quite shattering?" Claire remarked facetiously. "I thought you two were estranged?"

"I know, but he's still my children's fa—"

"How much money do you need?" Claire cut in.

Mrs. Hughes looked confused.

"I really don't need..." she attempted. "But it's true, madam. I can't bear it anymore!

I'm finally on my own!"

"How's that again?" Claire asked. "What? What can't you bear? Tell me!" she demanded.

"Well...my Jimmy and his baby sister barely get by between my salary and the money my husband sent each month," Mrs. Hughes began. "Now that James Sr. is gone, I must find a position that pays more or even two jobs." Tears streamed down her face. She then looked into Claire's eyes and continued. "Mrs. Rogers, you've been incredibly kind to let my little Jimmy spend so much time with Camille. But

I must leave your beautiful family to earn more. And God knows I don't want to do that!"

Beloved by rich and powerful friends, Claire was loathed by workers for her austere ways. Constant clashes with disgruntled employees reinforced her demanding and heartless image. Feuds with investors over stock shares also resulted in highly-publicized lawsuits. But for Claire, overcoming challenges was just part of the game. One step at a time, she told herself. Claire knew how to play the corporate game better than any male executive who worked for her. Employees like Mrs. Hughes were dispensable. Except in this case.

"Whatever do you mean?" Claire pressed.

"I mean that little Cami will be devastated!" answered Mrs. Hughes.

Claire sat in silence, considering the repercussions for her little princess. Camille was about to be abandoned by her surrogate mother, if truth be told, and by her best friend. Idly standing was not an option.

"I see," said the matriarch in a stern voice. "Very well, we will have to work this out, Mrs. Hughes," she continued. "Why don't you go back home for a few days...sort things out at the village...and let little Jimmy stay here as long as it takes. Meanwhile, I will increase your salary and give you additional responsibilities. Do you understand?"

Mrs. Hughes was filled with gratitude.

"Yes, madam," she replied humbly. "I do, madam."

"Damn it, Mrs. Hughes!" Claire said aloud. "You know how I feel about people breaking up their family."

Overcome with emotions, Mrs. Hughes kissed Claire's hand.

"God bless your soul, madam!" she said excitedly, praising her. "God bless you and your family! Merci beaucoup!"

"You may leave now," Claire dismissed.

"Yes, ma'am. Of course."

Respectfully, Mrs. Hughes distanced herself, then exited the door.

CAMILLE AND JAMES

Monte Carlo: 1971

8

In the months that followed, the Rogers shared quality time typical of an idyllic family. Jacques and Claire were an enviable couple both in their public and private lives. Camille refused to think about the night Jacques entered her room. If she told her mother, it might rip the family apart. Burdened with a terrible secret, unable to tell a soul—even James—was a steep price to pay for a child.

Both mystifying and terrifying, Jacques had either forgotten about the incident or was more aware than he let on. Camille buried and compartmentalized her thoughts. Jacques was an adoring father. Jacques did something bad. Jacques couldn't have done something bad because he adored her. Although she fought tears nightly, her pain, confusion, and silence were worth the sacrifice as long as she made her mother happy.

* * *

Claire was performing strange rituals in her chapel that even her local priest did not condone. Her personal brand of fervent religiosity was overshadowing, even eclipsing, her family life. But on December 24th, at six o'clock in the evening, Christmas spirit filled the Rogers Home. A sweet, earthy smell was coming out of chestnuts roasting in an open fireplace while the fully decorated house beamed with wreaths, garlands, hollies, glittering ornaments, and fabric bows. An adorned fifteen-foot live Christmas tree with elegantly wrapped presents underneath stood near the blazing fireplace. Guests would be arriving momentarily.

Claire searched room to room for Camille.

"Camille darling, where are you?" called out the matriarch. "Hurry along now, dear! Our guests will all be here soon!" she continued. "I want to make sure you're dressed up properly for church!"

Claire and her family traditionally attended the midnight mass to celebrate the birth of Jesus Christ. Participating in such activities was a must. And since it was their favorite holiday, Camille and James were more than happy to comply. While Claire continued to look for her daughter, Mr. Thompson appeared.

"Oh, Mr. Thompson! There you are! You gave me such a fright." She then composed herself. "Have you seen little Cami?"

"No, madam," answered Mr. Thompson. "I imagine she's up in her bedroom?" "Of course," Claire agreed.

Claire encouraged Camille's artistic talents and her creativity, even if it meant too much time spent alone in her room. She and Jacques firmly believed that artistic endeavors provided the balance she needed to succeed. Upon reaching the upstairs hallway, Claire immediately heard Camille's voice and smiled contentedly. Tiptoeing into her room, she realized that Camille was playing with her dolls. At her first glimpse, she saw nothing out of the ordinary, so she drew herself closer. Camille, with her back against the door, was immersed in roleplaying with her porcelain Ken and Barbie dolls, unaware of her mother's presence.

"Hello, sweetheart. I've missed you so much." Camille said, holding the Ken doll as she mimicked Jacques' voice.

"Go away, you disgusting little swine!" a repulsed Barbie replied. "You're nothing but an evil monster! I want you to get lost! NOOWWW!"

"But I just want to say goodnight to my little princess," begged the Ken doll.

"Please let me touch you, my little sweetheart? I want to hold you so badly. We'll cuddle up together, my angel, and fall asleep. Wouldn't you like that?"

"You don't care about me!" The Barbie lashed out. "You lie to Mommy, and you lie to me! You lie to everyone! This dagger will purify your evil soul!"

Camille then pretended to stab the Ken doll, thrusting a mini dagger straight into his stomach.

"Ahh! But I love you," the Ken doll dropped to the floor.

"Didn't I warn you to stay away from me?" she raged. "Jesus doesn't love you! I HATE YOU! I HATE YOU!"

Claire stood aghast, shaken to her core. She instantly knew Camille was recounting an event with Jacques in lurid detail. Sensing someone at the door, Camille turned to discover her mother, white as a ghost.

"Oh, mother!" stammered the little girl. "I-I didn't mean to..."

Claire's eyes darkened with the damnable look of a woman betrayed. Marching angrily toward Camille, she pinched her by the ear, dragging her like a cat out to the hallway. Camille was filled with terror, unable to defend herself.

"How dare you?" she exclaimed furiously. "How dare you!" she shrieked, louder now. "After all that I've done for you, this is how you repay me? I am your mother, for God's sake! Damn you! Stay right where you are, young lady!" She abruptly left the room.

Minutes rolled by. She returned with a buckled belt in her hand. Claire was now on a rampage, knocking vases and valuable arts along the way. When Camille saw the belt, she shuddered. Horrified beyond belief, she scurried into a corner, trembling in fear. Claire hunted Camille down and hit her several times in the arms, legs, and back.

"PLEASE! Mummy! Don't!" Camille shrieked in pain, letting out a horrifying scream. Still, the anger continued.

"And that's for keeping this a secret from me!" Claire exploded. Her voice then dropped to a whisper. Borrowing a line from Eleanor of Aquitaine in "The Lion in Winter," she declared, "I can peel you like a pear, and God himself would call it justice," her eyes drilled into Camille.

Camille suddenly learned the hard way how unfair life could be. Claire's cruelty was the vilest act she had ever been exposed to. The mother she loved and trusted turned her heavenly kingdom into a hell on earth in an instant. Unable to escape her mother's wrath, she felt a warm sensation trickling down to her leg. Paralyzed with her fear, she urinated in her underwear, rendering her helpless. As Claire raised her hand to hit her again, James suddenly appeared, tried to grab the belt, and desperately begged Claire to stop.

"No, Mrs. Rogers! PLEASE!" he pleaded. "Don't hit her again!"

But James swiftly took a hard blow from Claire. Slapping him across the face, she threw him into the corner next to Camille, who watched in horror. Blood slowly dripped from his torn lips. And with absolute hatred, she declared, "May you both rot in hell for this."

Seconds later, Mr. Thompson arrived on the scene, trying to catch his breath. The moment Camille saw him, she bolted out of the room.

"Mrs. Rogers!" he said. "Is there anything I can do here, madam?"

To his dismay, he saw James bleeding on the floor. Camille ran to the dimly lit chapel and locked the door behind her. Scents of ancient relics filled the room while the burning aroma of candles and incense infused with vanilla, jasmine, oak, and berry spice wafted through the sanctuary.

Camille instantly felt a sense of peace as she kneeled below Christ. She had considered this place holy since she was a little girl. The extra room turned house chapel, where members of the Rogers family—including Mrs. Hughes—prayed to cleanse their souls, was now Camille's saving grace. Like her mother, she sought absolution for her sins. Baby Jesus, Mary, and Joseph nativity figures rested beneath the altar.

She sat down on a church pew, heedless of her pain. Overcome by guilt for leaving her best friend to suffer alone, her heart pounded, and she could barely breathe. A multitude of unanswered questions swirled in her mind. She closed her eyes and whispered verses from the Holy Bible.

"Even though I walk through the valley of the shadow of death, I will fear no evil," she panted heavily. "For you are with me, your rod and your staff, they comfort me, and I will dwell in the house of the Lord forever. Amen."

Intermittently, Camille rushed to the door, peered through the crack, then returned to the pew. The more whipping, the worse the cry for help.

The rising decibels made her feel helpless to a point she could not bear. Tears rolled down her cheeks as she took it all in.

"The LORD is my shepherd; I shall not be in want," she prayed. "He makes me lie down in green pastures; he guides me in paths of righteousness for His name sake."

At that moment, Camille felt the earth move as if a burden had been lifted from her shoulders. She suddenly felt mysteriously protected. She was deeply humbled by this experience.

Back in the hallway, Mr. Thompson stood powerless.

"You stay right there!" Claire threatened. "Just stay right where you are."

Jacques then entered the room, afraid of what he might find.

"What is going on here, Claire?" he pressed.

"LEAVE! NOW!" Claire commanded Mr. Thompson.

Nervously scramming like a stray cat, Mr. Thompson immediately left the room.

"BUT Claire!" reasoned Jacques. "It's Christmas!" She stared at him blankly but did not utter a word. The two returned to their Christmas guests. It was the least they could do.

* * *

James—bandaged up, lying on his side inside his bedroom—stared blankly at the bare wall after the house doctor came to visit the following morning. Suffering cuts and bruises, a broken arm, and a dislocated shoulder, his impassive face was purple and swollen. His body was covered in contusions. Mrs. Hughes sat quietly beside him. Disheartened, Mr. Thompson tried to comfort her.

"This can't happen again, Mrs. Hughes," he said somberly. "She's taken this way too far. Breaking little Jimmy's arm like that—I really don't know how much more I can take. And to think, she didn't even give you the raise she promised after Mr. Hughes died, that Mrs. Scrooge! All she does is abuse people! The woman carries so much hate within her!" He then added. "I swear, I'm calling the police if she does it again."

In deep shock, Mrs. Hughes remained silent. Her inconsolable heart, unbearably heavy, cried out for her son. Watching him lie there motionless ripped her heart apart. She blamed herself for not being there for him. Yet leaving the Rogers Estate with two children to support is not an option in her mind. A soft knock at the door. Camille, wearing a long sleeve turtleneck top and jeans, waited by the door, her face also bruised.

Mr. Thompson took a deep sigh and let her in. "Hi princess," he greeted her tepidly.

"How is he?" asked Camille.

"He's not talking. He's in pain."

Camille headed straight to Mrs. Hughes.

"Mrs. Hughes, I'm sorry about Jimmy," she said regretfully. "I brought these for you both." She handed over a gift basket filled with luscious fresh peaches. Camille never thought her mother would lay a hand on her, let alone someone else's child. She could not defend her mother's inexcusable actions. Nevertheless, she still loved her. Mrs. Hughes, with swollen, bloodshot eyes, smiled weakly without saying a word. She and Mr. Thompson quickly left the room. Camille moved closer to James' bedside.

"Merry Christmas, Jiminy Cricket!" she said. "I prayed for you at church today." She hesitated. "I know Jimmy...I know you tried to protect me," she added in a sober tone.

Stoically facing the wall, James was emotionless. Camille gave him a tight hug.

* * *

The following evening, the Rogers resumed normal activities and Mrs. Hughes helped Camille with her evening bath. But the moment Mrs. Hughes lifted Camille's arm; her heart skipped a beat. She saw bruises on her arms, neck, legs, and back, which explained why she wore a long-sleeved shirt and pants when she visited James. It was a heartbreaking scene that told a disturbing tale.

"I hope Jimmy will be better soon," Camille said.

"I will bring him your love," Mr. Hughes replied.

"Yes, send him my love!" Camille lit up. "So, you think he'll be OK soon? I'm making a pretty basket for mother's birthday, and I want him to help me." Then in a sober voice, she continued. "Mrs. Hughes?"

"Oui, mon amour? Yes, love?"

"You think mummy's still mad at me because of papa?"

Mrs. Hughes broke a painful smile, trying to hold back her tears. Struck by Camille's unconditional love for her mother, her eyes were tender but sad.

"No, dear, of course not," she sighed. "I'm sure that Jimmy will help you with whatever you need." But Mrs. Hughes did not believe her son would do anything for Claire ever again. It was long past time to plan an exit.

"And watch our favorite movies before bedtime, right?" In total denial, Camille returned to her singing. "Pomme de Reinette et Pomme d'Api..."

That evening, a fight erupted behind the closed doors of the Rogers' master bedroom suite. Claire cursed her husband for "touching" her child, while Jacques blamed Camille for the misunderstanding—Camille's fantasy life in overdrive, he argued. Hurling insults at one another, vases and expensive figurines flew across the room. Their harsh words escalated. Camille listened from her dark bedroom with the door left ajar. Terrified by the havoc, she curled up on the bed, clinging to her bunny. Horrified by the crashing sounds, she was overwhelmed by the fear that mommy might leave daddy.

* * *

Several years later, the lavish chateaux had turned into desolate walls and dismal loneliness. The once happy home was now a fortress for Claire's saintly piety. Receiving high marks on her report card from private homeschooling, Camille raced across the living room to bring her mother the good news. Sipping her usual afternoon tea while Mozart played in the background, Claire was reading the Bible.

"Mother! Mother!" said Camille, handing over her card. "Look at what I achieved—straight A's!"

But Claire was unmoved. Cold as ice, she gave her a quick glance and then returned to her reading.

"Mother, will you look? Please?" Camille begged. "I received the highest score on my final test today. Isn't that wonderful?"

"I don't care, Camille!" Claire lashed out. "You and your evil stories have ruined this family!"

Camille began to apologize profusely.

"I'm sorry, mother! I didn't mean to..." she responded in despair.

"Mean what?" retorted Claire. "You can't even say it, can you? Get out of my sight! GO ON! GET OUT OF HERE!" she shouted.

"I'm so sorry mother! I really didn't mean to ruin..."

Camille was utterly distraught by her mother's reaction. She left weeping, running into James, whose hands were loaded with gardening tools for Mr. Thompson. He was doing his best to avoid Claire.

"I'm sorry!" she said frantically.

"Are you OK?" James asked.

Their eyes locked, sharing once again that horrible incident from when they were younger.

Camille was bitterly silent. James watched as she rushed upstairs and slammed her bedroom door.

The diamond mogul had lost her way. A demanding employer who ruled with an iron fist, she ran both her company and home through intimidation. Notorious for inflicting pain on her "enemies"—including staff who disagreed with her dictums—she took pride in disciplining people while exerting control over their lives. Making people suffer in unfathomable ways, they willingly accepted her nefarious ways as their new normal. Sadly, she did not feel an iota of guilt about her actions. Her paranoia mounted daily; Claire was a deeply suspicious person.

Jacques walked into the living room. "She's only trying to make you happy, Claire," he tried to reason. "Give the kid a break! You're way too hard on her. And it wouldn't hurt to lower that DAMN pride of yours either!"

"Awww...isn't that sweet—JACK?" She remarked, dripping with sarcasm. "Shouldn't you be out molesting babies and spending my money?" she added. She then rose from her seat and gracefully walked away.

* * *

Claire became increasingly withdrawn over the next several months. She refused to make important business decisions, abused drugs prescribed by her doctors, and relied on alcohol to cope with her emptiness and loneliness. Her bedroom was cluttered with important documents, folders, journals, books, and papers, along with prescriptions and whiskey bottles—as if the room had not been cleaned for months. Carrying a silver dinner tray for Claire, Mrs. Hughes knocked twice on the bedroom door. Camille trailed close behind.

"Mrs. Rogers?" she said. "I brought your dinner, madam. It's time for you to eat." A depressed Claire donned in her nightgown slowly rose up from her bed, struggling to make it to the bathroom.

"NO...Go away!" she yelled out, mumbling to herself. She then swallowed a cocktail of drugs, chasing it with a glass of water from the sink.

Mrs. Hughes and Camille turned away from the front door. The two were walking away when they heard a sudden thud.

"What was that?" wondered Mrs. Hughes aloud.

"I don't know," Camille replied.

"We better check, my dear."

"Mrs. Rogers! Are you all right, madam?" Mrs. Hughes asked anxiously. "Your door is locked!"

"Mother! Are you OK?" echoed the teenager. "Could you open the door, PLEASE?"

Not a single word from Claire. The two began to panic.

"Mrs. Rogers? Can we come in?" pressed Mrs. Hughes again.

Taking matters into her own hands, Mrs. Hughes used her spare key to unlock the door. They hurriedly entered her room only to discover the diamond magnate lying on the bathroom floor, completely unresponsive.

"My sweet Lord! Mrs. Rogers!" Mrs. Hughes shouted frantically as she tested her breath. Turning to Camille, she cried. "RUN! Go get Mr. Thompson! Tell him to call an ambulance now! HURRY! PLEASE!"

Camille stared at her mother's lifeless body.

"Mother, please! Wake up!" she screamed. "I can't leave! I can't! Is mother fine? Is she going to die? TELL ME! TELL ME!" she demanded.

Ambulances with flashing lights and police cars soon took over the circular driveway. The police captain and his lieutenants closed off the room with yellow tape. Two Emergency Medical Technicians tried to resuscitate the lifeless body. Unable to detect a heartbeat, they rushed Claire to the nearest hospital in Monaco. But it was too late. Camille was grief-stricken, as though someone had cut her heart out. Fear of the future overwhelmed her. The golden years her mother perpetuated were tragically cut short. Who would love her now? Who would protect her? She clung to Mrs. Hughes. Mrs. Hughes, Mr. Thompson, and Jacques responded to questions raised by the police. Who found her? What was the time exactly? Who was in the room? Did she receive threats from anyone? Jacques sat in a wide armchair, his eyes red with tears. James leaned against a wall. He wanted to hug Camille, to tell her that things would be alright. Yet he remained at a distance, unable to speak or move. In truth, James was glad Claire was dead.

JAMES AND CAMILLE

Paris: 1997

9

Pulsating Paris—known for its art, fashion, gastronomy, and historical influences—was livelier than ever. For many, the city of lights was a haven for café cultures, designer boutiques, romanticists, and lovers. For others with a keen eye for creativity, Paris was a playground for artists perfecting their craft.

As a red Ferrari roared down to the world-famous Champs-Élysées, onlookers tried to catch a glimpse of the driver. Minutes later, the Ferrari entered a parking lot reserved for dignitaries. A 16th-century palace (once the royal residence of King Charles V) stood just a short distance away. This historic landmark, known as The Louvre, is the largest and most diverse museum in the world—home to countless Greek sculptures, Egyptian artifacts, and great artists like Michelangelo, Leonardo da Vinci, and Rembrandt. Tourists easily lose their way, taking days or even weeks to walk through the enormous collection of thirty-five thousand pieces.

James Hughes, now in his late thirties, was the mysterious driver of the eye-catching Ferrari. Sporting a pinstriped suit, fedora hat, polished dressed shoes, and dark sunglasses, he looked more like a gangster than an aristocrat. James is a talented artist in his own right. Removing his sunglasses, he glanced at the car mirror. *You can do this*, he thought to himself. He took a deep breath before slipping out of the car. Gripping a black leather portfolio, he scurried down The Louvre's marbled hallway into a pyramid-glass skylight lobby packed with tourists.

Cristel Adams, a young American intern whose fluency in French and Italian landed her a coveted museum post, met James in the lobby. Wearing a dark turtle neck and skirt, comfortable shoes with black nylons, and a pair of thick black glasses, she cheerfully waved him forward. A dignified tubby Parisian in his mid-sixties with sparse gray hair approached them. Museum Director Monsieur Bernard Delacroix had sole authority over the museum's art collections and exhibits, though, in principle, he answered to a board of directors and to the museum's fundraising committees. Delacroix was Cristel's primary supervisor.

"Bonjour, James!" Cristel nearly shouted. "It's so good to see you. I would like you to meet my boss Monsieur Bernard Delacroix."

James reached for his hand.

"How do you do, sir?" he asked politely.

"Monsieur Delacroix, Monsieur James Hughes is the artist we discussed," Cristel continued.

"Bonjour," acknowledged Delacroix with his heavy French accent. "So you're the promising young man I've heard so much about."

James chuckled, then replied. "Not exactly so young, but that's very kind of you, sir. It's an honor to meet you."

"James' work is exceptional," Cristel explained. "I think he would be the perfect candidate for your consideration."

Delacroix looked confused.

"...as a candidate for our September Artist of the Month exhibit in the contemporary art department," she reminded.

"Oh yes! Yes, indeed!"

Delacroix turned to James and apologized in French. "Je suis désolé, James. It's been one of those weeks."

"Pas de problème," answered James.

Cristel continued. "His black-and-whites are complex yet mystical. They leave one craving more. It's truly a remarkable body of work. See for yourself Monsieur Delacroix!"

James savored every word. "How incredibly kind of you, Cristel," he blushed, then looked to Delacroix. "I tell you, sir, you have a keeper here. We met last summer at the Prince's reception in Monte Carlo. We've been in touch ever since. She's been so kind."

"Yes, she told me," replied Delacroix. "You have a great future ahead of you, young man!" he complimented. "Shall we go inside and take a look at your masterpieces?"

"My masterpieces," James smiled excitedly. "I'm very much obliged, sir. Oh, but wait," he halted. "I brought a guest. She's only a few steps away."

"A girlfriend perhaps?" jested Delacroix.

"My sister," James replied.

"How considerate," Cristel remarked. "Don't you agree Monsieur Delacroix?" "Yes, yes, indeed." He said. "So she's your sister?"

"Well, sort of..." James answered absently while scoping out the lobby. "She can't be too far. Let me introduce you both, if only I can only find her."

"Would you like me to call security to assist?" offered Delacroix.

"No, no," James declined. "That won't be necessary. She'll turn up."

A short while later, James found Camille quietly staring at a painting by her favorite French impressionist, Pierre-Auguste Renoir. The stunning masterpiece was a beautiful oil painting of "Mademoiselle Irène Cahen d'Anvers"—or "The Little Girl with the Blue Ribbon"—that reminded her so much of herself when she was young. Bequeathed to Camille by her mother, who sold it to the Louvre Museum after Camille disobeyed her one day.

Now in her late thirties, Camille had acquired a taste for the finest things money could buy, in keeping with her blue-blooded background. Beautiful and svelte, glamorous and sophisticated, she was also intensely private. Camille was, above all, an enigma. Her best childhood friend, James Thomas Hughes, remained her closest confidant.

Camille wore an elegant Chanel dress contoured to her body with a matching mini-bolero jacket and black-laced gloves. Wrapped in an expensive mink stole, she was elegantly accessorized with impressive diamond jewelry. Her subtle L'Allure perfume drifted through the lobby. Delacroix was immediately smitten by her irresistible charm and beauty, even from a distance. Heat rose from his belly to his forehead. Sweating profusely, he nervously dipped into his pocket for a handkerchief and dabbed his forehead. It was a strange reaction for a world-class curator who had confidently handled more important dignitaries and powerful figures than he could count. He was having a hard time controlling an urge to bed this exotic woman.

"Camille! There you are!" called out James. Oblivious to her surroundings, Camille heard the distant sound of her name. "What?" she whispered absently, slowly turning to him.

"I'd like to present to you Monsieur Bernard Delacroix," James took a deep breath. "The gentleman in charge of the exhibit and his highly competent assistant, Ms. Cristel Adams," he added. "They've been kind enough to consider me for their upcoming 'Artist of Month' program here. Isn't that wonderful?!"

Camille snapped out of her reverie.

"Oh, I must apologize. Bon-jour," she explained in an elegant voice as she turned to them. "It is my absolute pleasure to meet you both. I was just admiring one of your pieces," she told the director.

"The pleasure is all mine, madam. Wait a second, you look familiar," he noticed. "Oh, that's because you're looking at the daughter of the jewelry titan Claire Marie Rogers—founder of the multi-billion euro company L'Allure," James elucidated, then added. "THE premiere luxury diamond jeweler in the world."

Delacroix turned to Camille and said, "Is that right?"

Camille leaned over and said softly, "I've heard the rumor as well. And it's mademoiselle, by the way. Not madam."

It finally dawned on him. "Oh, that L'Allure!" he exclaimed. "Yes! I've heard of them," he teased.

Everyone laughed.

"Well, now," Camille said. "Let's get back to business." Slipping back into silky spoken French, she asked Delacroix whether his work was going well. "Enchanté...comment vont les affaires?"

When Camille reached out to shake Delacroix's hand, he brazenly stuck his finger into the palm of her hand.

"Nice to meet you, sweetheart." Delacroix winked lasciviously, then added, "Your brother is quite talented."

Camille stiffened and immediately pulled back her hand. Her pleasantries ended as fast as her rage accelerated. She was quietly mortified but maintained her composure.

"Gross," she uttered.

An awkward silence followed.

"I'm sorry?" pretended Delacroix.

"You will be, you tub of lard," Camille retorted smoothly, unable to hold herself back.

She then gracefully walked a few feet away and lit a cigarette.

Delacroix's primitive sexual advance stunned her. Not only had he insulted her, but he was in direct violation of the museum's sexual conduct protocols, a fireable offense. Frequently exposed to repulsive behavior by men, Camille was unforgiving. Moreover, unbeknownst to Delacroix, he had just offended the newest member of the museum's board of directors.

James was shocked by her hostile behavior toward Delacroix. "My God, Camille! What's the matter with you?" he chided aloud. "Apologize to the man!" he insisted further.

"Not with that swine, I won't," she quipped while puffing her cigarette.

Embarrassed, James turned back to Delacroix nervously, trying to make amends.

"I'm sorry, Monsieur Delacroix," he said sheepishly. "Camille is just um, uh...um," he stammered.

"It's OK, James." Delacroix smiled. "Don't worry about it. Perhaps the lady is just having a bad day?" he suggested. "C'est la vie."

"Indeed!" Convinced that this colossal blunder would cost him his single greatest opportunity, James continued to plead with Camille, hoping she would budge. If Delacroix raised this encounter with the board, all would be lost. Camille's rude behavior could blemish his record as an upcoming artist or kill his career altogether. But to his great surprise, his efforts quickly paid off. Camille finally relented and agreed to apologize.

Waving her hand to Delacroix as a sign of peace, Camille gave him a warm smile. He reciprocated with an even bigger smile. While still waving, however, she flipped him the finger, along with an insolent smile. Delacroix was shocked. All were taken aback. Oddly still, Camille placed an order with the first servile-looking person she saw, a dark-skinned man wearing a printed silk Sherwani top.

"Monsieur, se il vous plait!" the heiress said aloud. "I'll have a Vodka Martini, darling. And oh, monsieur...no olives, please. Merci beaucoup!" she smiled and turned away. The man was flabbergasted.

"Pardon?" he asked with a French accent, not sure what to make of it.

"NO o-live," she enunciated harder in French. "Got it, darling?"

The stranger shook his head and ignored her. He instead rejoined his family, who stood waiting to start their tour just meters away.

"Oh, how rude!" remarked Camille. "What a shame."

A towering security officer approached from behind her. "You can't smoke here, madam," he cautioned in his deep baritone voice. "This is a non-smoking room—voir les signes," he pointed to the nearest sign. "All rules must apply."

Refusing to turn around, Camille muttered under her breath. "Ain't that the truth." She then faced him. "Gladly, officer." Her eyes slowly traveled from his head to his feet. A look of disgust rolled over her face upon realizing she was facing a version of Delacroix. "Whatever you call yourself," she added condescendingly. A tourist holding a souvenir cup happened to walk by, and Camille dropped in her cigarette. Both the officer and the tourist were mystified.

Struggling to divert the group's attention, Delacroix changed the subject.

"Your sister?" he asked cheerfully. "You don't resemble one another."

"Oh, that!" James acknowledged. "It's a bit complicated. Camille is not... well, she's not my biological sister. We grew up together in the same house. I knew her family well...she knows mine. We're like siblings. Does that make sense?"

Delacroix nodded slowly. James continued, "She was adopted when she was just a baby. And the rest was history. Funny, how that works out, isn't it?"

Turning to Cristel, Delacroix responded, "Imagine that."

"It happens, Monsieur Delacroix," she smiled.

"So the board has a new member?" Delacroix asked Cristel, trying to change the subject. "Do you know who that might be?."

"I spoke with our C.E.O. Monsieur Durant yesterday. He directed me to arrange your meeting with James, but he didn't mention the new board member," Cristel responded.

Said Delacroix, "I heard it was someone who was intensely private with a high-ranking position from the French Riviera and a woman..."

"Oh my God," Cristel reacted softly.

Delacroix realized that Camille fit the description. "This means she asked our C.E.O. to arrange the meeting with James," he muttered as he pieced together the chain of events.

"What's going on?" James interrupted.

Delacroix gave Cristel a sobering look. "Forgive my ignorance, James. But our newest board member turns out to be...well, your sister."

"Is this a joke?" His eyes darted from Delacroix to Cristel, then back to him again. "But I thought Cristel arranged our meeting."

Cristel cut in regretfully. "I didn't think it was important so long as you met Monsieur Delacroix, and he agreed that your work should be exhibited."

James was astonished to learn that Camille was behind the meeting. Just when he thought he finally made a connection on his own, it could not have been farther from the truth. Nor did it help dispel Camille's repeated warnings that he was incapable of making it in life without her—a confidence-crushing reality.

"I don't believe this..." a deflated James said absently.

Delacroix quickly moved away from James, eagerly embracing other guests in the room. He feared that he would pay a steep price for his clumsy sexual handshake with Camille.

* * *

Driving back through the familiar streets of Paris to Camille's private villa in Avenue Montaigne, James brooded in silence. Wondering how he might have prevented the disastrous meeting, he concluded there was little he could have done. Bridging the gap that quickly went sour between Camille—the source of his livelihood—and Delacroix, who held the key to his future, was a long shot. Although Camille might exert power over Delacroix as a board member, she should stay out of his business. Moreover, as the museum's director, Delacroix could still prevail. James finally broke his silence. His tone was casual, but Camille sensed that her response was important to him.

"That wasn't cool what you did back there, Camille," he started, with sadness in his voice. "They were going to give me the break I've been waiting for," he hesitated. "I'm not sure what will happen now after that fiasco," he continued, shaking his head. "The most famous museum in the world wanted my artwork, and you just blew it for me." James gave out a deep sigh.

Camille was expressionless. She remained silent as though she had not heard a word he said. Reaching down into her pocketbook for a compact, she powdered her nose and face using the car mirror, then touched up her lips. Minutes passed. James pulled into the parking lot of a run-down bistro, a dingy joint in the outskirts of Paris he frequented during his visits, and turned off the car engine.

"And what exactly is the meaning of this?" a very surprised Camille asked.

"It's been a long day, and I'm hungry," he replied.

Camille looked at him askance, taking her gloves off. "And I suppose I should be thankful to you, your Highness?" she responded dryly.

"Well, not everyone gets to be a queen like you," teased James. "Oh, come on, Camille! Don't be so overly dramatic. This place is not that bad," he reassured. "They have a great 'liver and onions' dish on the menu. The one you like, remember?"

"That is precisely why I dread going back to this God-awful place—REMEMBER?" she countered. "Besides, overcooked food is not my idea of a good time, darling. You know that."

"That's right. Come to think of it," he began to ponder. "They do tend to overcook their food here. You would think that if anyone would get it right, it's the French."

"Not all French, darling," Camille responded. "But unlike mother," she began to reminisce. "She would never allow such a thing." She then paused. "Life might have been different if only..."

"Here we go again." James interrupted. "Camille, we've been through this a thousand times already. Just drop it now, OK? Your mother overdosed on pills she was taking for God knows how long, ended up on a stretcher, and was pronounced dead upon arrival at the hospital. That's it! End of story! What more can I tell you?" He then calmed down and continued. "Look, that crazy woman has finally set us free, OK? Good riddance! You should be happy about it. Now, can we please go in and eat before we both pass out from starvation?"

James believed in moving forward in life. Rehashing the past was counterproductive. Inevitably, he would have to snap Camille out of a bad mood or pull her out of another deep depression that could stretch for several weeks, triggering unrelenting grief and hopelessness. Protecting Camille was like caring for a delicate flower or a helpless animal. She required his fullest undivided attention, as if her life depended on him. It was a monumental responsibility. James had to remain focused and at her disposal, whenever necessary, for both to survive.

"So, are we going in?"

Surprisingly, Camille agreed.

"All right, darling," she said animatedly. "Let's have a delightful meal at your favorite place."

The two then slipped out of the car and marched into the nearly empty bistro.

Minutes passed. A French waitress came out of the kitchen. James immediately flagged her down.

"Bonjour!" greeted the waitress with a thick French accent.

"Bonjour! Pour deux se il vous plait," James said, indicating for two guests.

"Par ici...s'il-vous-plait," she ushered the two to a table. "How are you two doing?" "Never been better, darling," Camille quipped bitterly. "And you, mademoiselle? Enjoying the place?" She smiled and then rolled her eyes, murmuring, "What a meaningful chat."

"Why don't you tell her how you really feel?" James said with annoyance in his voice.

"Darling, if I told people what I really think of them, I'd be in jail by now," she quipped.

"She's just being nice, Camille. Just being nice," reasoned James. "That's all."

The waitress returned to their table with menus. "Well, here we go," she said. "I'll be back to take your order."

"Merci," said James. The two sat opposite each other in a cheap burgundy leather booth with visible cracks.

Minutes flew by. The same waitress returned to take their order.

"So, are you ready yet?" she asked. "What can I bring you?"

Fully engaged in reading the menu, James was still vacillating on his order. "I'm still debating whether or not to have the burger with fromage or my usual croque monsieur," he said.

Camille studied him for a moment. Then slowly forcing his menu down with one finger, she remarked in her trenchant voice. "I want to go home now, that is, if you don't mind."

James turned to the waitress and said. "I'll be ready after she orders."

"Very well..." she said to the waitress. "I'll have your bloody liver, please." "Excusez-moi?" the waitress asked.

"You're excused, darling," said Camille while glancing at her out-fit. "Well, maybe not in those clothes you're wearing, I'm afraid," she added dryly. "Darling, who dresses you?" she asked.

"I'm not quite sure what you mean," she replied.

"You're going to need a lot of help mon chéri," Camille continued. She then pulled out her personal stylist's business card and said, "Here, call Mademoiselle Bertrand. Tell her I sent you. If anybody can perform a miracle, she can."

The woman turned red, clearly flustered. Clearing his throat, James cut in. "Pardon, the sideshow. But what mademoiselle Rogers meant was liver and onions, cooked rare. Se il vous plaît?"

The waitress gave a sigh of relief.

"D'accord...pardonnez-moi!", she smiled. "And you sir?"

"I'll have your hamburger after all. Rare as well."

The waitress returned to the kitchen. Soon thereafter, they had their dinner, paid the bill, and drove away into the night.

* * *

Claire left very specific instructions in her Last Will and Testament. If anything should happen to her, her Trust lawyers would immediately take over her daughter's life. Camille was soon enrolled in Switzerland's Institut Le Rosey, one of the oldest and most expensive boarding schools in the world. Known for distinguished alumni such as Prince Rainier of Monaco and Prince Albert II of Belgium, movie stars like Elizabeth Taylor and Sir Roger Moore sent their children to study there.

But Camille had lost everyone she loved: her mother, Mrs. Hughes, James, and Mr. Thompson. Sinking into deep bouts of depression, she soon became withdrawn from the world around her. She was next shipped off to Harvard University to complete her college and business degrees. Constantly missing her best friend James through all those lonely years, she often wondered if fate would bring them back together. Enduring a litany of psychologists, psychiatrists, and prescription medications during her darkest days, she never once lost hope of reuniting with James.

James returned with his mother to the Provence village, where his maternal relatives resided. For years, he bounced around France, Italy, and Greece—wherever Mrs. Hughes could find work. One winter night, his mother had a brain aneurysm and passed away. He then visited his father's grave in Wales and went to London to find his estranged sister, who had run off with her high school sweetheart when she was just a teen.

That was the last anyone had heard of James until Camille—suffering from another downward spiral—moved back into her mother's chateau. A week later, James joined her and slowly nursed Camille back to health. His very presence gave her the will to live. Brother and sister, friends or lovers? The lines were beginning to blur.

Camille decided to renovate the Chateau Estate while significantly reducing her house staff. Carefully selecting furnishings and artworks that conformed to her personal taste and style, the project continued for two long years. Maintenance workers, gardeners, florists, and handymen were constantly on site. On rare occasions, Camille brought in additional staff for dinner parties and special events. But no one was permitted to enter the main house without her explicit permission.

James managed the property, supervised the staff, attended to Camille's personal needs, and whatever else she wished of him—which was no easy task given how difficult she could be. Then again, the challenges empowered him. He felt resilient. James was trusted by a deeply broken woman who relied on no one else. Their rekindled relationship brought back warm memories of their childhood. And the newly renovated chateau had never looked more regal.

* * *

The morning following their visit to The Louvre, Camille awoke to a gloriously sunny day inside her luxurious master bedroom suite. Featuring gold-inlaid furniture and draperies in rich, elegant colors, her bedroom was modeled after Queen Marie Antoinette's palatial Versailles bedoire.

The fragrant scent of jasmine, roses, and other flowers permeated the air. Birds chirped in unison as they clung to the Versailles-like pedestal railings on the grand terrace balcony. Slowly removing her elegant diamond-studded eye cover, Camille stretched her body and took her time to rise. She then put on a silk robe and slipped into mink-furred bedroom slippers. As Camille headed down the ornate sweeping stairwell, an elegant black feline, appropriately named Prince, followed right behind.

Camille stepped into a meticulously manicured French garden with a rich array of exotic flowers, plants, and trees. She closed her eyes, took a long deep breath, then slowly released it while counting from one to ten. Camille was exhilarated. The warm sun and fresh air of the French Riviera offered hope and promise for the new day. She quietly snipped off a baby pink rose and laid it down to a winged cherub centerpiece around the corner. Professing her faith in a sacred manner, she began to pray. Minutes later, she entered the gourmet kitchen where James was having breakfast, reading a photography magazine.

"Bonjour, mon chéri!" a cheerful James greeted her, then spotted the cat. "There's my little Prince!"

"Morning, darling," Camille said.

She poured herself a glass of freshly squeezed orange juice, gathered her prescription pills, and swallowed them.

"You're all spiffed up," she noted as she reached across the counter for the remote control and turned on the television. "What's the occasion, darling?"

"Nothing in particular, really," James replied. "I was just going to..."

The screen went from a fuzzy picture to live news. A major international news station was breaking a developing story: the body of John Doe had just been unearthed by the Beverly Hills Police Department in California. The crime scene had all the markings of a homicide, according to the detective in charge. Camille was riveted.

"I'm sorry, darling...what did you say?" she responded absently.

"I have to run errands today before the maids arrive," James reiterated. "Which reminds me...I must buy food for your little Prince."

Brisk video footage showed a telegenic female correspondent interviewing an eyewitness. "Where did you find the body...and can you tell us what happened here sir?" asked the reporter as she lifted the microphone to his face. "And more importantly, were you afraid, sir?"

"You can say that again!" the attention-loving teen answered.

"Yeah, me, my dad, and my dog Goober usually like to hike early in the morning," he began to recount his story. "Then I saw Goober wagging his tail like crazy. Like he's never been so excited in his life, you know? But then, when I got closer—WHOA, NELLY!" he exclaimed.

The gruesome discovery of John Doe's body in rigor mortis left everyone shaken. "Anyway, the stench was so overpowering that I was dry-heaving!" the teen continued.

Camille was now glued to the television screen. "What did you say again, darling?" she asked.

"I said, I've got a couple of errands to do today," James repeated. "And I need to buy food for the cat."

James quietly observed Camille for a moment. Then switching his voice to a much deeper tone mimicking the reporter, he said.

"It was reported today that the largest estate in Monte Carlo, believed to be the home of a jewelry heiress, burned to the ground. Camille to earth—earth to Camille? Anyone there?" he teased.

"Sshhh!" she admonished as she continued to watch.

"Oh-kay!" James whispered.

Minutes later, James was engrossed in the news. The same female reporter was now chasing after the lead detective.

"Detective! Detective! Could we speak with you for just a minute please?" she pressed.

Detective Evan Carter of the Beverly Hills Police Department was a hard-nosed temperamental fellow in his early fifties. He and younger partner Lieutenant Drake Monroe had been after the same serial killer for several years now.

"Detective, we understand that the body was found by a hiker early this morning, who then alerted the Beverly Hills Police Department," she said. "Does the BHPD have a plan of action, and has the victim been identified?"

"A teen hiker," corrected the detective in a sharp tone.

"I'm sorry, detective?" a confused reporter asked.

"You said...a hiker," Carter continued. "It was found by a teen hiker and his father at around six this morning...in that order."

"I see," she smiled faintly, turning back to the camera.

"I don't think you do, miss," he quipped. "It will take some time to determine the name since the body was just discovered a few hours ago. The rest is yet to be determined. That's all we have for now."

"I'm sorry, one last question, detective," she insisted.

"Shoot."

"People are speculating that this is the work of the serial killer."

"Well, we don't know that yet, do we now?" he cut in quickly. "The perpetrator hasn't gone public, so you shouldn't either. Again, we have to await the Los Angeles Coroners' autopsy report for a positive identification. Then and only then, we'll compare notes with other agencies and intelligence partners to determine if it is indeed our guy. This is the procedure. Thank you."

Carter's public disdain for the media was well documented. He thought reporters were a bunch of opportunists who seldom got their facts straight.

The media rarely gave him the credit he was due. Instead, they continued to criticize his department with anything they could pin against him. Seething, Carter suppressed his anger and walked away. "When are you people ever going to learn?" he muttered to himself.

Camille and James glanced at each other, then shrugged it off.

"That poor thing," Camille commented.

CARLTON

Washington, DC: 1965 – 1999

10

Special Agent Joe Carlton was a man of principle. His keen investigative mind and brilliant interrogation methods had won him the respect of colleagues throughout the Bureau, including when he was recognized by a sitting president, Ronald Reagan. His team had solved countless complex murder cases—tracking down notorious killers, fugitives, and even the criminally insane.

Carlton grew up in one of the toughest, high-crime neighborhoods in Brooklyn, New York. His father was a factory worker, and his mother was a part-time seamstress. They struggled to put food on the table and clothe their children. Once Carlton set his mind on a goal, he could care less about the consequences or what anyone might think of him. He was a tough and independent survivor. Tall and slender, with dark hair and attractive green eyes—in his early 60s—and women still found him irresistible.

Carlton understood at a young age that he could not rely on his parents for financial support. To put himself through college, he worked at a variety of jobs—as a dishwasher, busboy, errand boy, and construction worker. He was accepted at the University of Virginia, where he met his wife and went on to study law. After achieving a law degree, he joined the FBI.

* * *

At two o'clock on a busy Friday afternoon, employees at the FBI Headquarters raced in and out of the revolving door, trying to complete as much work as possible before the end of the week. A special task force gathered in an open-space office on the third floor. Photographs of suspected killers were pinned on the wall.

Carlton was distracted. His marriage was crumbling, and his beloved daughter was wasting away from a debilitating illness. On his way home, he stopped by a local bar. By his seventh shot of Jack Daniels, Carlton felt even more hopeless, but at least the whiskey dulled the pain.

Hours later, his wife Maureen—an abrasive middle-aged Italian whose face had taken a beating over the years—stood by the front door in her nightgown, seething with anger. "Where have you been, Carlton?" said Maureen in a contemptuous voice. "We've waited for you for four freaking hours! Have you no decency even to call us, you SON- OF-A-BITCH!" She hesitated, then added. "Congratulations for being the worst husband and father in the world!"

Carlton turned to his wife. "You certainly haven't changed much since I left you this morning, dear," he retorted dryly, slurring his words. "But your hair is a tad blonder. You're a thing of beauty—you know that? Just quit ragging on me, WOMAN!"

He grabbed a blanket and a pillow from a hallway closet, threw them on the couch, and went around a corner as his wife continued to badger him. Entering his daughter's cozy bedroom, he noticed her pink bedside lampshade was still on. The room was plastered with various teen idol and movie star posters.

Carlton was a devoted, nurturing father and a stabilizing force for his daughter. The two were very close. Spending quality time together and participating in school activities, Carlton took an active role in his daughter's life. He attended Parents and Teachers Association (PTA) meetings, campus recitals, and contests, as well as other school activities, and picked her up from school every Friday.

He took his daughter and her close friends for ice cream and often drove them to the movies. Carlton was a wonderful father, but lately, work demands were dominating his time. He was also badly off his game. He missed three of his daughter's doctor appointments, including one where both parents were specifically required to participate. Nevertheless, she would always be his beloved little girl, and he would watch over her for as long as God permitted.

His daughter Jesse, a fourteen-year-old redhead with sparse freckles on her face, was a straight-A student and a star athlete during her grammar school and early high school years. Previously full of life, an advanced illness was ravaging her body and spirit.

Tucked into bed, she smiled contentedly as her father walked in, as though she had been expecting him at that very minute.

"Hey, sweetie. You're still up!" Carlton said as he sat by her bedside. "How was your day?"

"Hey, daddy. It was fine," replied the teenager. "We missed you today."

"I know, sweetie..." he replied in a regretful tone. "I was tied up at work again. I'm sorry." He reached for her hand and added. "I just want to say goodnight, and I love you."

"I love you too," she reciprocated. "Well, goodnight."

"Goodnight," he whispered.

Fighting back his tears, Carlton turned off her bedside lamp. He rose and quietly closed the door behind him.

AMANDA AND TAYLOR

Nice ~ Monte Carlo: 1985 – 1999

11

Through the cacophonous din of a busy Nice International Airport one morning, two Midwesterners from Los Angeles emerged at the street level. Taylor Collins—a pretty honey-blonde, blue-eyed fourteen-year-old with an appetite for life. She stood next to her mother, who could barely contain her excitement. Amanda Collins was a single parent in her mid-thirties. She acted more like an older sister than a guardian, although a loving one. She and her daughter bore no resemblance.

Mother and daughter moved to Los Angeles from Mount Vernon, Virginia—a small town popular for art festivals, cozy restaurants, and quirky boutiques. But young Taylor had her heart set on Hollywood stardom. Because her philandering father was absent for the better part of her life, her mother spent most of her days trying to make up for it. She gave her daughter whatever she wanted within her limited financial means, spoiling her rotten with pleasure. Living in a small apartment on the seedy side of Los Angeles, Amanda signed her daughter up for a summer camp attended by children of the rich and famous.

While the two waited in line for the next cab to arrive, Amanda and Taylor were ecstatic. "Oh-my-gosh! I can't believe we've finally arrived, mama!" the teen said, then giggled. "Can you believe this?"

"Oh yes, I can!" Amanda replied with a Midwestern accent. "And who knows, you might even meet a cute boyfriend this time," she continued.

"Then you can finally get away from that weirdo next door; what's his name again? Heck! You know, our neighbor!"

"Mama! Don't be such a Debbie-downer!" Taylor said aloud. "We're in France now, remember? I heard on TV once that there are about sixty billionaires living in Monaco. So, guess where we're going next, mother-dear?"

Amanda looked appalled.

"And what? Have an average age of about three hundred and about fifty illegitimate children from twenty different mothers all waiting for their inheritances? No thanks! YUK!" she revolted. "What's wrong with you, young lady? Besides, I don't like Italy, my dear. So there!"

"It's not Italy, mamma," Taylor corrected. "It's Monaco! Check your map! Geez, where have you been?"

Minutes later, a male cab driver in a Mercedes yellow taxicab pulled over. He popped his trunk door open and came out to assist with their luggage.

"Bonjour!" greeted the driver with a heavy French accent.

"Bun-shour, mister!" replied Amanda in an amateur-sounding accent.

The two then jumped inside the cab, as did the driver. They left the crowded airport and drove into a busy highway, where hideous traffic brought them to a halt. Amanda leaned forward to the driver and handed over a piece of paper with the hotel address.

"Um, mister, we're going to...the Star Hotel by the water, please. Do you know the place?" she asked.

"Oui, oui," the driver nodded in agreement. "Je sais où cela se trouve!" he said, explaining he knew exactly where it was.

"Perfect." Taylor smiled.

"Anyway...I don't want old guys for you, either." Taylor continued. "I'm talking about men who might have broken a few hearts here and there but are now ready to settle down."

"Listen to you," Amanda interrupted.

"Men that are very wealthy but lonely," Taylor added. "Men who are heirs to their parents' vast fortunes and are now looking for the love of their lives. And you have to have love," she said adamantly. "Take a look at Prince Albert II, for instance. He's handsome, charming, and very RICH!" She then smiled and let her mind go.

Amanda gave her a disapproving look.

"Oh please, I don't mean him either," she continued. "Besides, what you got on him anyway? He's been doing a lot of good lately."

"Uh-huh," Amanda hesitated.

"I'm serious, mama! Why do you think I begged you to take me to Europe? Because I want to develop my artistic talents and learn about European history and culture. And if I play my cards right, then maybe..." she began to act regal. "Just maybe...I could become the next Grace Kelly someday!" She then turned to her mother and continued in a British accent. "Would you like me to sign an autograph for you, madam?"

Amanda understood that getting into the movies had now become her daughter's life's mission. Looking her straight into her eyes with a smile, she said. "Oh, honey...you really want this acting badly, huh?"

"Uh-huh..." Taylor cracked a smile.

"Well then, we're just going to channel your inner Grace Kelly!"

The two laughed it off.

* * *

Two hours later, Amanda and Taylor found themselves settling inside a fleabag hotel called "Star Hotel" on the outskirts of Nice, miles away from the great restaurants and famous shops. It was the only hotel Amanda could afford. Overrun, dilapidated with infested hallways, there was no manager available to greet them. Still, the two were happy to be in France. Taylor sprawled across the bed on her stomach, listening to music through her headphones while reading a French fashion magazine. Amanda unpacked their luggage.

"Taylor, you need to call your cousin George today," her mother reminded. "Tell him we've arrived, so they know we made it." She then repeated. "Don't forget to call today—all right?"

"Yes, mama. I said I'll do it later today," Taylor replied nonchalantly.

"I mean it!" Amanda snapped.

"Geez, Louise!" Taylor startled. "Ms. Grouch with no pouch! I thought we were on vacation, mama!" she replied. "I didn't realize I've traveled with the Gestapo police!" "Oh, hush!" her mother said. "I just don't want you to forget about it. That's all." "OKAY-OKAY! But I heard you the first time," reasoned the teenager. "You don't have to repeat yourself, you know. Could we get a burger soon? I'm starved."

Amanda tossed over a box of cookies she bought at the airport.

"Here, have some of these for now. It'll be hours before we get to the other side of town."

"Bummer...very cute, mama," Taylor quibbled quietly.

* * *

Later that day, the mother and daughter duo rode in an overcrowded train from the beautiful city of Nice to the glamour town of Monte Carlo. Forty-five minutes later, they arrived at the train station. They were immediately enthralled by the extraordinary surroundings as if stumbling into a dream. They walked in awe on Princess Grace Avenue, admiring extraordinary surroundings everywhere they turned—wealth, beauty, style, and glamour—everything Monaco has to offer.

From elegant designer shops to the famous Café de Paris bistro in Square Beaumarchais plaza, Amanda and Taylor reveled in delight as they moved closer to the Harbor. First, they passed the three-star Michelin restaurant Le Louis XV run by famed chef Alain Ducasse inside of the historical Hôtel de Paris. A few steps away was the world-famous gambling house of Casino de Monte-Carlo, the venue for James Bond and other major motion picture productions. Walking the thoroughfare, they had a stunning view of the Monaco Harbor filled with lavish mega-yachts. The stark contrast between that world compared to Amanda and Taylor's simple lives could not have been more sobering for the two. Deciding to have a quick snack in a less expensive bistro, Taylor stopped to buy a magazine from a nearby newspaper stand. "Gosh, mama! I could live here forever!" Taylor grinned, flipping through the pages.

"Me too, honey! Me too," replied Amanda. "Boy, were you ever right about this place. It's gorgeous!"

"I told you, mama! Anyway, see this?" Taylor pointed to a column in the magazine. "This magazine is going to give me my BIG break. You can come along too if you like," she added proudly.

"Come along?" Amanda asked quizzically. "Let me remind you— you're only fourteen, remember?" she added. "What is it anyway?"

"Oh, it's an audition."

"Well, let's see!"

Flipping back the pages, Taylor read the advertisement to her mother.

"Here it is!" she said. "Attention! Calling all female actresses between the ages of fourteen to twenty years old: We are currently casting a lead role for an upcoming big-budget film. You must be ATTRACTIVE, TALENTED and PROFESSIONAL. To audition, please call the number +(377)747-0000. This is your once-in-a-lifetime opportunity to star in a movie—CALL NOW!" Taylor pondered for a minute, then continued. "Attractive, talented, and professional. That's me, mama! Did you bring our phone card?" she asked.

"Oh, shucks!" Amanda recalled. "I forgot it at the hotel! Darn it! Let me see." She began to think. "I thought I saw a public pay phone out there earlier. Maybe we could charge it back home, that's it!" she smiled. "We'll charge it back home! You've got to call them now, sweetie! No time to waste, but wait!" she halted. "Shouldn't you be auditioning back in Hollywood, where we live?"

Taylor's undeterred voice insisted. "We're here now, mama! LET'S GO!" Locating the nearest payphone, Taylor dialed the number while Amanda listened in.

An answering machine immediately responded with a slightly bizarre welcoming message from a woman with a perfunctory sounding British accent.

"Welcome. You have reached Bright Lights Productions," the voice began. "If you're calling concerning the audition, please leave a detailed message, and someone will get back to you with further instructions. It is very important, however, to state your name, when you'd like to audition, and, more importantly, to leave your number. Otherwise, it'll be very hard to find you—wouldn't it?" The voice then softened to a whisper. "Remember, you must be acquiescent to this project...BEEP."

Amanda and Taylor could only giggle.

"Ah, yeah...Bon-jour." Taylor began.

"Ak-wi—WHAT?" Amanda interrupted from the background. "What does that mean?"

"Mama!" Taylor chided, covering the speaker phone. "It means close, OK?" she reassured her proudly as though she had given an appropriate answer. "Doesn't it mean to agree?" Amanda guessed.

"Then why ask mama?" she whispered sharply, then continued. "Um, this is Taylor, Taylor Collins," she continued. "I'm calling about the audition. I want to be a star!" she chuckled. "I mean, I just got into town from LA, and I'd like to try for the part. Anyhow, I'm staying at the Star Hotel in Nice; you can call me there. I mean, I'm not there right now. But the number there is +33 4 93..."

Monte Carlo was already a whirlwind of fun for Amanda and her daughter Taylor.

* * *

On the other side of town, James carefully parked his gleaming silver McLaren with alloy wheels on the side street. He leaned against his car, had a quick smoke, then flicked it to the ground before crossing the sidewalk. Moments later, he entered a sleek-looking black building, passed through lobby security, and took the elevator up to the penthouse. One of the first properties Claire had acquired back in her deal-making days, and among the highest priced real estate in the world, the building was located in the heart of Monte Carlo. It was now solely owned by Camille.

As the corporate headquarters for L'Allure, the building also housed the Rogers Foundation and Camille's film production company. James overlooked the business affairs department for all three. Although not an Ivy League school graduate, Camille trusted him. And that was good enough for James. Settling inside his office, he read letters and messages left by his secretary. He checked his voicemail, returned a few business calls, spoke to Camille about a pressing matter, and met with the staff. Several hours later, he left the building carrying a bag of mail and several packages. He loaded them in the trunk and drove back home.

* * *

The following day, Camille was grating imported cheese on the kitchen counter. The scrumptious smell of an American macaroni and cheese dish baking in the oven permeated the air. James, in a jovial mood, placed a stack of mail and packages on the kitchen table.

"Bonjour, mademoiselle!" he greeted. "Here is your long-awaited mail." He then noticed the dish cooking in the oven.

"Hhmm...that smells yummy, mon chérie! Is it Mac and Cheese—I dare say?" "Oh, hello, darling!" Camille glanced up. "Yes, indeed, your favorite snack." "Wonderful!" he rejoiced. "I feel like today is my birthday."

Having taken private lessons from her godfather, chef Paul Bocuse with no success, Camille's idea of "cooking" is to heat up dishes in the oven, topping them off with expensive aged cheeses, and would still be quite proud of it.

"Did you just return?" Camille asked. "Yes, I purchased a new lens for my camera," James replied. "It's been acting up lately. Oh, I almost forgot!" "What?"

"Someone responded to our audition ad," he continued. Can you believe it?" "Well, did you do us the courtesy?"

"Nope."

"Why not?"

"I didn't know what time to schedule." He responded, grabbing an apple from the table. "The call was from a teenage American girl and her mother. I doubt that they're serious."

"And you could tell all this by listening to just one phone message?" Camille remarked.

"I think so. You know how people are," he continued. "Like your mother used to say...always keep a straight appointment," he said. "Or was it, keeping appointments will keep you straight," he vacillated. "I never could quite get that right."

"Oh, shut up, you babbling fool!" Camille cut in. "I want you to call back and invite them for an audition here at seven sharp tomorrow night. Are you listening?"

"Yes, ma'am!" James replied.

"Then the four of us will go through the audition, have dinner and celebrate afterward!" she continued charmingly. "And James, only what we talked about, got it?"

"As you wish, my queen," he teased. "Please, give me a break. I know the drill. I'll place that call later today when I'm out and about." Then he added in a British accent. "Anything else, meh lady?"

"No, dahling!" Camille replied back, mimicking his accent, smiling. "You have been marvelous today!" Then returning to her normal tone, she said. "I'll let you know once your dish is ready, all right, my darling? This will be a perfect night!"

James replied nonchalantly, "I'll be in my office if you need me," and strode down the hallway.

* * *

Two days later, a train pulled up to the platform in Monaco. Taylor nearly bounced out the door; a backpack hooked over her shoulders. Amanda carried a tote bag in one hand and a map in the other. Wearing casual clothing, both were ready to tackle the audition of a lifetime. To be invited to a French chateau by the sole heiress to one of the world's wealthiest families was a dream come true. But to audition for a starring role in a movie was beyond anything they could have imagined. Filled with apprehension, Amanda and Taylor knew this event could easily change their circumstances overnight. But like typical tourists, the two immediately got lost, trying to find their way. Quickly re-doubling their efforts to make up for the lost time, they asked locals for directions. Trekking up the mountain for what seemed like endless miles, Taylor and Amanda were exhausted. Taking swigs of bottled water, they finally sat down at a resting station and suddenly noticed the area was practically a ghost town. Not a single soul was on hand. Unperturbed, Amanda dipped into her bag, pulled out a pack of cheese curls, and snacked at them as though it was just another day at the park while Taylor peeled a Starburst candy and began to chew it crudely. They resumed their trek up another empty road before finally reaching a cul-de-sac. Amanda quickly grew disillusioned.

"So, this is it?" a very frustrated mother asked. "The BIG Hollywood producer who's going to put you in the movies you've been talking about?" she mocked.

"No, mama!" Taylor reasoned. "They told us to go to the top of the hill and then a few more meters, OK?"

"A few?" exclaimed Amanda. "There's nothing close to us within a mile's range, sweetie! It's the end of the road. Not to mention, we are now, well, lost." She then let out a big sigh and added soberly. "This can't be good."

"But that's what it says right here, mama!" insisted Taylor. "We can't quit now. We've got no choice but to follow the instructions they gave us. Just hang in there, mama—PLEASE?" she implored. "I promise, we're almost there, and we will find it— OK?"

Amanda could only smile back, and on they went. It was now nightfall. The deeply ravishing orange sky was folding into darkness when a massive black-and-gold gate suddenly appeared before them. The two were now looking at the newly revamped Versailles-like French Chateau Estate of Camille Rogers. They were utterly breathless. The sprawling palatial chateau was beautifully maintained.

"Oh, my," said Amanda.

They looked to each other, then screamed in unison.

"Good Lord SWEEET, JEE-SUS!" Taylor exulted. "We're here, mama!"

"I sure can see that!" Amanda, still shaking her head, was trying to process the scene. "What are they—GA-ZILLIONAIRES?"

"Maybe more!" touted Taylor. "Maybe a whole lot more!" She then added. "I told you, mama!"

"You sure were right, honey!"

A stately gate inscribed with a twenty-four-carat gold leaf "R" stood before them, along with security cameras on each side. Taylor noticed a security phone attached to the sidewall. After a few rings, James answered from the speaker phone.

"Bonsoir?" he greeted.

Taylor, chewing gum to calm her nerves down, replied nervously. "Um, Bon-soir. It's uh, Taylor Collins. I have an audition tonight with um..." She haphazardly looked down at her crumpled paper and continued. "With um, Cam-Cam-il?"

A brief silence went by as they waited for an answer. The two had never been so nervous in their lives.

"Oh, yes, of course!" James finally acknowledged. "Please walk up to the front door, and she'll meet you there. I'll buzz you in," he instructed.

"Oh, OK." Taylor hesitated.

Within seconds, the majestic gates swung open to the kingdom of riches. Timidly, the two entered. Walking up to a circular driveway, both mother and daughter gawked at the surroundings. Minutes later, they stood in front of red lacquered double doors. Taylor immediately rang the door twice. Camille opened the door wearing a chic Chanel outfit and a lengthy diamond necklace, smoking a cigarette on a short holder.

"Well, hello, my darlings! Bonjour!" she greeted fervently. "And welcome to Monaco." Camille turned to Taylor. "You must be, Taylor Collins. Enchanté, mademoiselle!" she continued.

"Yes ma'am," Taylor replied.

"And you, madame?" she turned to Amanda next. "Who might you be?"

"Oh, this is Amanda," Taylor jumped in. "She's my um...my, my manager? And my mother," she hesitated. "Anyway, the person who called said I could bring someone with me."

"Oui, Oui. D'accord." Camille concurred.

Amanda, mesmerized by Camille's appearance, continued to stare blankly at her. "How'd you do, ma'am?" she said timidly. "You sure are pretty."
Amused, Camille smiled back.

"That's very kind of you, darling," said the heiress. "Well, it's an absolute pleasure to meet you both. Oh, good heavens!" she exclaimed. "Pardon my manners, but please, do come in! This is a big project, and we have a lot to cover in this audition."

Camille ushered her guests into the formal salon. Amanda and Taylor were stunned by the paintings, sculptures, and expensive furnishings. "This is amazing, Camille!"
Taylor said excitedly. "I still can't believe you invited us here! It's incredible. Seriously—thank you!"

"You're so sweet, darling," Camille replied. "I tell you what, this house..." she began to tell a story, "was built in the 1930s, and it once belonged to my mother. Thirty years later, during the Kennedy years, I revamped it."

"Wait a minute!" Amanda interrupted, her eyes widening. "You're not that adopted child of what's her face name...I mean her mother," she turned to her daughter.

"Hello?" Taylor replied. "Her last name is only Rogers. It's Claire Rogers, mama!"

"In any case," Camille continued. "My partner Monsieur James Hughes, who you will meet in just a moment...James darling!" she began to call out. "Our guests have arrived! Come and meet the girls! We're in the living room!" She then turned back and added. "And believe me, the renovation wasn't a bed of roses."

"Yeah, but you guys are super rich!" Taylor reacted. "What do you have in here anyway—DIAMONDS AND GOLD?"

"Taylor!" Amanda warned.

"Yep! It's a mansion, all right!"

"Oh, it's fine, darling," Camille said dismissively. "That's what this audition is for—to get to know one another. I simply want to determine if your daughter has the talent for a lead role in our big-budget film. If she's truly got the je ne sais quoi, what do they call them? The 'IT' thing. That's all." Then looking straight at Taylor, she asked. "Now, how does that sound?"

"YES! Please!" Taylor replied animatedly. "Really? That's all?" she added.

"Well, there might be just one caveat," clarified Camille. "My partner must test you on camera as you would expect. After all, it is a standard practice in the movie business. It's called the screen test. Besides, I don't see anything that'll compromise that right now." She turned back to Taylor and jested. "Or is there?"

Taylor blushed subtly.

"If you both are so inclined after he's done, I'll give you a personal tour of the house," she continued. Camille then looked to Amanda and asked. "Are you interested in acting, too?"

Amanda instantly shied away, unable to handle the attention. "Who...me? Oh, no!" she replied nervously. "I'm not an actress. My daughter is the talent in the family."

"But of course, you can act," insisted Camille. "Just be your natural self. There's nothing to it, really. The rest, I assure you, will fall into place. I promise. Do it for your daughter. It'll be fun," she encouraged further. "Besides, the gentleman who's doing the test is quite a lovely man. You'll like him."

Taylor gave her mother a begging look. In walked James, right on cue.

"You're talking about me again?" he teased.

All three gave a good laugh.

"Yes, darling," Camille replied. "Indeed, we are. Young ladies, may I present to you my business partner, my colleague, my dearest best friend, and brother, Monsieur James Hughes."

"Hello," Taylor greeted politely.

"Nice to meet...wait," Amanda halted. "A brother?"

"Almost," clarified James. "Well, actually, to put it in perspective, I'm the brother she never had. But we've known each other since we were kids and grew up together. So, are you girls enjoying yourselves?"

"Uh, yes, sir! Thanks!" the mother and daughter answered.

"Come to think of it, darling, why don't we show them the house before we proceed to the studio for the screen test?" Camille suggested. Besides, we'll all be hungry for dinner by then. Don't you think it's a splendid idea?"

"Yes! Please!" Amanda and Taylor answered in unison.

"Sounds like a game plan to me," James agreed.

A short while later, the group descended into the subterranean garage packed with exotic cars.

Taylor was stunned beyond belief. "Look at all these expensive cars, mama! Gosh!"

How many are there? Forty, fifty?" she asked.

"Good Lord!" Amanda agreed. "This is insane!"

"I'd say about fifty-five right now," answered James.

"Geez! You could feed a whole farm with that money!" Amanda blurted out. "You serious, mama?" said Taylor, rolling her eyes.

James and Camille chuckled. Camille next introduced the grand ballroom with massive French crystal antique chandeliers, an indoor pool and a large heated outdoor pool, the expansive patio garden with its tantalizing view, and the tennis court. They finally headed upstairs to Camille's luxurious master bedroom suite.

"No way this is a bedroom, Camille!" exclaimed Taylor. "It's a Marie Antoinette suite of Versailles, that's what! I've read about it in a history book, you know." "I'll say!" Amanda agreed. "And made fit for a queen!"

"So, you do know your history books after all," Camille smiled at Taylor. The group moved down to the hallway.

"Although," Camille continued. "I have a better idea for you, my darlings." She stopped dramatically in front of the next door. "And finally, my all-time favorite room, which had saved me from many of my troubles over the years." Gracefully swinging the double doors open, she presented. "Voila! My sanctuary! THE entrance to my heaven!"

Amanda and Taylor were slack-jawed in amazement. Camille's private jewelry collection featured some of the most expensive jewelry in the world. A treasure trove of unique diamond pieces worth hundreds of millions of euros glittered from every corner far bigger than Elizabeth Taylor's collection and private museums combined. The room was adorned with French tufted chase lounges, ornate vanity mirrors, and hanging chandeliers. Camille took a puff of her cigarette as she watched the scene unfold.

"Un-freaking-believable," a captivated teenager said breathlessly.

"It all started with my mother's love for jewelry auctions. She collected special pieces here and there when she traveled around the world." Camille explained. "But I've added a few of my personal touches over the years."

"That means she bought a whole lot more since then," clarified James.

"Are they real?" Taylor asked.

"As real as the blood pumping through your veins, darling," Camille answered nonchalantly.

Amanda was so stunned that she could only sigh. She stared at the magnificent collection with rapt attention.

"Remember when we used to play here, Cami?" James reminded. "After our long baths?"

"Oh, I remember," Camille recalled. "I remember it very well, darling. We both hid in the closet. Mother went crazy looking for us. Oh, what a great time we all had, didn't we, James?" Her smile then slowly faded. "Yeah, I miss those days..." Camille was adrift in her own reverie.

All three then quietly clattered down the hallway, giving her privacy.

"Camille! We best get on with this test if we want to finish," said James. "It's getting late!"

But Camille remained silent.

"Camille becomes sentimental when she talks about her mother," he explained. "She really misses her. And honestly, I can't blame her."

"Oh, we totally understand," Amanda sympathized. "Is there anything we can do?"

"No-no," James said. "I know the woman better than she knows herself. She just needs time. But enough about her," he concluded. "Let's just move down to the studio and take care of business. Would that be all right? I'm worried about our timing. I think we're cutting it close."

"It's all right with me," Taylor eagerly agreed.

"Film production starts next month, and we're on a tight deadline," James revealed. "Camille!" James called out to her again. "We'll just carry on for now. I'll get the girls started! Just come down when you're ready."

"Go ahead, darling!" Camille answered. "I'll catch up soon! I'm really sorry!" "Don't worry about it!" he reassured her. "No trouble at all!"

Turning back to the girls, he smiled. "I hope you girls brought your appetites." "Appetites?" repeated Taylor. "I'm so hungry; I could eat a horse!" "Taylor!" Amanda admonished.

* * *

A short while later, the three entered an audition room—a professional mini-movie set studio with state-of-the-art gadgets and the latest equipment. Taylor salivated over autographed photos from movie stars like Joan Crawford, Elizabeth Taylor, Richard Burton, Rita Hayworth, and so many others displayed in gold frames on the walls.

"OH MY GOSH!" Taylor exulted. "You guys know these people?"

"Yes, I'll even let you in on a little secret," James responded. "They're all personal friends of Camille," he informed.

"No way!" Taylor said, grinning from ear to ear. "Man! You guys are the coolest!" she looked to Amanda. "Aren't they, mama?"

"So true!" said her mother.

Ten minutes later, James went through his checklist for proper lighting and accurate positioning of his equipment. He was ready to roll the film.

"Ready, steady, and—action!" he shouted.

James began to film while Amanda and Taylor exchanged their lines, interspersed with laughter and giggles.

* * *

An hour passed. The smell of the dishes cooking pell-mell in the kitchen permeated the entire house. Camille was nowhere to be found. Expensive heirloom French copper cookware and baking equipment simmered on stove tops and double ovens. Two of Camille's part-time French maids worked tirelessly as they wrapped things up, getting ready to leave.

"Mais nous ne sommes pas encore fini? Qui va nettoyer tout ça?" one maid asked, concerned about who was going to clean up after them.

"Je ne sais pas. C'est ce qu'elle a dit. La femme est folle," explained another, saying she did know and that Camille had lost her mind.

Amanda and Taylor returned to the living room giddy and exuberant. They were anxious to share their experiences with Camille. "Camille! We're back!" James called out. "We've finished the screen test! The girls did great! Where are you?"

After a brief silence, Camille replied, "I'll be right there, everyone!"

The lights dimmed in the living room, lobby and balcony as if an event was about to start. They gave out murmurous sounds. A drum roll followed. Standing on the mezzanine balcony, a huge spotlight dropped over Camille. Emerging ever so glamorously resembling Joan Crawford, she began to recite words uttered by her in "Mommie Dearest."

"I'd rather be here with you...than anywhere else in the world..." she said proudly. "You, all of you, here and everywhere...gave me this wonderful evening tonight. And on behalf of myself and Mr. James Hughes, we accept it from you, and only you—I LOVE ALL OF YOU!"

Camille, deeply immersed in her character, had transformed herself into a movie star of the Golden Age of Hollywood. Her demeanor had changed. Her look was uncanny. She was now Joan Crawford. Amanda and Taylor were spellbound. James, pretending to be a paparazzi, grabbed a vintage camera off the side table and began to take snapshots of Camille.

Minutes later, the lights returned. Camille gracefully descended the grand sweeping staircase. Like a true ardent fan, James began to clap proudly, encouraging the girls to follow him. Camille halted in front of them and pulled a cigarette from her diamond-crusted case. James, dipping into his pocket, rushed to light her cigarette.

"Here you go, my love," he tendered.

Camille took her first puff. "Thanks awfully, darling," she said to James then turning to Amanda and Taylor. "Well, well...if it isn't my girls."

Awestruck, they continued to gawk at the stunning heiress.

"So, shall we experience the most exquisite dinner?" Camille asked.

"Oh my God, Camille! You look amazing!" Amanda broke her silence, turning to her daughter. "Doesn't she, honey?"

"Yeah, you do, Camille! You really looked incredible!" "That's my girl!" boasted James.

"Merci beaucoup. How very kind of you all," Camille smiled. "Everyone, please follow my lead."

* * *

James, along with their guests, trailed Camille to an opulent dining room featuring an elongated table seating thirty guests, matching French-antique dinnerware, and massive chandeliers—the most beautiful room Amanda and Taylor had ever seen. A grand feast awaited them. Among the culinary delights were mouth-watering classic gastronomic French dishes, including Escargots à la Bourguignonne, seared Foie Gras Terrine, seafood crème emulsion appetizers, and Duck à l'Orange glazed with sweet orange sauce. A delectable Roast Beef with Bordelaise sauce and French-cut Crown Roast of Lamb stood out with dishes like Cream of Corn Soufflé, Roasted French Potatoes, and a tempting rosemary aroma.

On the other end of the table, a section of elegantly decorated cakes and pastries included Crème Brûlée, Crêpe Suzette, Apple Tarte Tatin, and colorful Petit Fours. A bottle of vintage Louis Roederer Cristal champagne—once hidden from the Nazis during World War II—sat in an ice bucket on an ornate stand, while martini cocktails and champagne flutes (along with an Apple Martinelli juice for Taylor) were all placed accordingly on the table. The feast was a masterpiece, the ultimate French dining scene.

James gallantly pulled out a chair for Camille, then offered the same to the girls. "Merci mon chérie," said Camille.

"Merci, too, James!" Amanda and Taylor chirped.

"I'd like to make a toast, please," Camille said, gently tapping her knife on the glass.

"We begin our glorious celebration by welcoming our lovely guests tonight, Amanda and Taylor Collins." Raising her glass, she looked to both mother and daughter. "James and I are thrilled to have you in our humble abode. Here's to a splendid evening! Bon appétit, my darlings!"

"Humble abode?" commented Taylor. "Not from where I sit!" she laughed.

"And to you, mademoiselle, for bringing your daughter," James told Amanda. "And last but not least..." He then looked Camille in the eyes and continued in a sobering tone. "To you, my love, for the unrelenting devotion you give to us time and again. For you are the life we breathe, the sun we live for, and the beauty we adore. We are humbled by your presence." He then raised his glass higher and added proudly. "You outdid yourself again, Mademoiselle Rogers!"

Camille was deeply touched.

"Thank you, my darlings!" she replied humbly. "What can I say? The pleasure is all mine. Cheers, everyone!"

"Cheers!" Amanda toasted her glass.

"Yay! Me too!" Taylor followed.

Amanda and Taylor, starving for hours, quickly gorged their food down.

"Très bien?" Camille observed, asking the girls if everything was fine.

Each nodded cheerfully. Camille then served Taylor her classic French Bordelaise sauce from a silver gravy boat named after the Bordeaux region of France, famous for its wine. It was a scrumptious demi-glace red wine made with a combination of bone marrow, butter, and shallots; known to pair well with red meat.

"You must try this Bordelaise sauce Taylor," Camille suggested. "It pairs very well with roast beef. You'll be pleased, I promise."

"Oh! A red gravy sauce!" Amanda reacted.

"It's Bordelaise sauce, mama. And it's French," Taylor corrected, embarrassed for her mother.

"Darn!" she cackled. "What is it, anyway?"

"Who cares, mama!" Turning to Camille, she continued. "My mom is a wonderful cook too, you know. That's why I like trying new stuff. She basically cooks everything I like 'cause I'm always hungry!"

Taylor, still with a mouthful, continued sharing her thoughts.

"Um, I have a question," she began. "This stuff we're eating? It won't kill us—will it? You know, like you see in the movies?"

Camille and James gave each other furtive glances, then burst into laughter.

"No, Taylor! That's ridiculous!" Camille said. "We're not that kind of people! You watch too many horror films, darling."

"Yeah, I suppose you're right," Taylor said.

"You just be quiet," Amanda insisted.

"What? What'd I do?" she replied innocently.

James abruptly rose and excused himself.

"Where you going, darling?" Camille asked.

"Pardon moi," he apologized with a faint smile. "Please excuse me, ladies. I'm feeling a little tired."

"Well, can we help?" asked Camille.

"NO!" James snapped, then loosened up as soon as he heard himself. "I mean, it's nothing. It's just that I might've caught the bug from last night." He smiled. "But um, you girls keep enjoying your meal. I'll be back before you know it."

"D'accord," Camille acquiesced. "Let me know if I can do anything—all right?" "Surely, I will," James said as he exited.

Minutes flew by. He returned to his seat, visibly relaxed.

"Feeling better?" asked Camille.

"Much better, thank you," James answered. "Now, where were we?" He picked up his black silk damask table napkin and placed it on his lap.

Mutely, Taylor stared at the cut to his right jaw, just below the ear, as blood slowly dripped on his shirt.

"So, how did you girls like your dinner?" he asked, seemingly unaware of his injury. "I bet there's nothing like this in Virginia, right?" he grinned.

Amanda looked quizzically.

"Hmm...where could that be now?" Camille said dryly.

"The Midwest," James said, stealing a glance at her. "Never mind."

Camille then noticed Taylor. "What is it, darling? Is everything all right?" she asked.

But Taylor remained voiceless; she continued to gaze at the bloodied cut.

"Taylor honey, you OK?" her mother asked. "What's the matter, sweetie?" She then looked at James, startled. "Oh, MY LORD!"

Reluctantly, Camille looked at James.

"Good heavens!" she exclaimed. "I thought someone died or something." Then she relaxed. "Darling, shouldn't you be stitching that up? It looks awfully bad from here, my dear" she paused. "You sliced yourself again, didn't you?"

James sat confused. Gradually feeling the side of his face, he realized he was bleeding. "Oh, geez! I guess so!" He arose yet again. "I'm sorry! I uh, cut myself from shaving this morning. It must've been deeper than I thought. I'll be right back."

James left the room one more time.

"You know, he must do a better job of taking care of himself," Camille said soberly. "The things people do just to get attention these days— Mon Dieu!" She then faced the girls and added. "I tell you what, his fifteen minutes of fame won't even last a minute! HA! How would you like that?"

Amanda and Taylor were at a loss.

"But what if he slices himself again?" stressed Taylor.

"Fine." Camille relented. "If it makes the two of you feel better," she called out for him. "James darling! The girls and I would like for you to come back now! The show's OVER!" she continued, then turned to both.

"He's had this nasty habit since he was ten. He says it's from shaving, but I know better," Camille nodded, pursing her lips.

"Really?" Amanda repeated. "Since he was ten?"

Feeling a slight intoxication, Camille began to ramble senselessly.

"I tell you," she started. "Those were some of the precious moments of our lives together. Cause if one has to do it, you've got to boot them,-knock them, shove them aside, and that's just the way life is!" she asserted. "You've got to grab hold of it so tight, taking each moment and putting them all away, you know?" Then she slammed her fist down on the table. "ARE YOU LISTENING TO ME—YOU TWITS?" Camille asked angrily, and rose up. "You girls better not leave this table until you both finish your dinner—GOT IT?" She warned, her eyes blazing with fury.

Amanda and Taylor sat in silence, completely powerless. They immediately complied with her strange demands.

"Yes, ma'am," they said nervously in unison, furtively glancing at one another.

As Camille stood, James entered the dining room.

"She's right, you know," He said, topping off their champagne. "It's important that you enjoy what you have now. Cause if you don't... YOU'LL BE SORRY!" he added in a sing-song voice. Clearing his throat, he returned to a more dignified voice. "I mean, while you still can."

Camille rolled her eyes, utterly bored.

"Back already?" she asked with a wry smile. "I'm going to powder my nose if anyone needs me." She then left the group.

* * *

A few minutes later, Camille returned to the dining room, surprised to find that everyone had moved to the next room. She entered the formal salon and saw Taylor lying on the couch, visibly shaken, her face turned pale.

"What happened to her?" Camille asked James.

"She didn't pay her taxes," he jested dryly. "I don't know."

"A little too young to get exploited by Uncle Sam—don't you think, darling?" retorted Camille. "Silly Thomas."

"Who's Thomas?" Taylor asked in her weak voice, gasping.

"Oh, that's James Thomas Hughes," Camille said. "You best rest up, darling. You really can't keep up."

"You mean when you're mad at me," James added.

"Hello? PLEASE?" Amanda interrupted. "There's something wrong with my daughter. Did anyone notice? Could we please get her to the nearest hospital, so I'll know what the hell is going on?"

"Very well," Camille agreed calmly. "Just follow the hallway to the living room. When you see a huge vase, make a right and, voila! You'll see the main door," she directed. "Bonne chance, mademoiselle." She then turned around, smoking her cigarette.

"No! That's not what I meant," a frustrated Amanda explained. "What I meant was us! As in, the three of us take her to the hospital—please? Look, I wouldn't even know where to begin."

"Oh, hush, darling!" Camille said. "It's probably nothing; you watch."

"Um, will you excuse us for a minute, Amanda?" asked James.

"Yeah, sure," she said.

James pulled Camille to the corner of the room, where they began to talk privately.

An argument ensued. Camille was incensed.

"And how am I to know what she is allergic to, huh?" she retorted. "Those simpletons can't even tell the difference if they're eating "foie gras" or their "Egg McMuffin" sandwich. I have no idea what you're talking about!"

"SSHH! Keep it down, will you?" warned James. "I don't think the entire neighborhood heard you."

"Well, you started it!" she replied sharply.

"I'm just saying...if it's possible, Camille." James countered.

Frustrated, Camille began to fire back in multiple languages.

"Je n'ai pas de temps pour ce non-sens. Peut-elle mourir déjà?" she dismissed, asking if Taylor could die already. "Because I say so! THAT'S WHY!" she roared. "Ho finito di parlarne," she said in Italian, telling him she was now done talking about it.

"That's it?" James said. "That's all you've got to say? Donc, ce est ça?" he responded back in Italian, hoping that God would help them all. "Che Dio ci aiuti, allora è cosi?" "James, c'est tout ce que j'ai mon frère! Comprendre?" Camille switched back to French, saying that was all she had.

"Enough already! This conversation is OVER!"

Taylor was coughing with labored breaths on the couch while the two continued to bicker in the opposite corner. Twitches and violent spasms flared up as she desperately gasped for air. Finally, Taylor collapsed to the floor, rolling next to the center table.

In the wake of her daughter's misery, Amanda screamed, "OH MY GOD! Taylor! Honey! Are you OK? Holy shit! We've got to take her to the hospital! NOW!" she shouted.

James rushed to the couch. Camille followed him.

"What happened here, Amanda?" he asked.

"I wish I knew!" she tried to explain, her voice trembling as tears streamed down her cheeks. "I had my arms around her, she was breathing fast, but the next thing I knew, she dropped to the ground. You've got to call an ambulance! PLEASE! JAMES! DO SOMETHING!" she begged.

"Dropped dead?" Camille asked coolly.

"CAMILLE—do you mind?" James said, annoyed. "We must save her!" He then placed two fingers on Taylor's neck, trying to feel her pulse.

"My God! She's got no pulse!" he said.

Gathering his thoughts for a moment, he tried his best to remedy the situation. But something about Camille's demeanor made him suspicious.

"Dammit, Camille! Did you...?" he asserted.

"DID I WHAT?" she cut in sharply. "If she's not breathing, that means she's DEAD, doesn't it?" Her voice grew powerful. "DOESN'T IT?"

"You've killed her!" Amanda howled. You killed my little girl!" She repeated frantically, then muttered to herself. "I have to call my mother...they're going to come out here." She then turned to them and bellowed. "THIS WAS SUPPOSED TO BE AN AUDITION!"

"Will both of you relax? PLEASE?" Camille stepped in calmly. "If we all just remain calm, we're going to get through this, all right?" Camille turned to Amanda and said, "Now, Amanda darling, listen to me carefully. Can you think of any food your daughter is allergic to? Perhaps some kind of prescribed medication she's taking? Basically, anything that might cause her to react this way? Anything at all?" she probed.

"I don't know. Maybe." Amanda hesitated absently. "God! What am I saying? I mean, yeah, she's terribly allergic to seafood. For emergencies, she needs one of those big old needle shots if it's really bad. But um, we haven't had any seafood tonight? Or have we?"

"Well, there you go!" Camille confirmed. "A simple seafood broth would easily cause this complication," she informed. "It'll slow down her breathing very much like an asthma attack followed by an attack in the central nervous system such as respiratory depression or what they call hypoventilation, and God forbid, a cardiac arrest. In worst cases—death."

Amanda almost passed out.

"Death?" she questioned.

"Yes—DEATH."

"This is not good," said James.

"But why can't we just call an ambulance?" Amanda insisted.

"Well, there's always the Princess Grace Hospital," Camille suggested. "But it's a long way from here. This is not America, my dear."

"And we're talking about a fifteen-mile radius," added James. "At a minimum!" Amanda began to panic. "No hospital nearby?" she asked nervously. "What if someone has an emergency like right now? Worse yet, what if people die for heaven's sake?" she added.

"Well, that's what James is counting on, darling," Camille said facetiously. "CAMILLE!" James admonished, shaking his head. "This ain't the time."

"Fine." She dismissed.

Camille walked between the two. "Stand back. STAND BACK!" she commanded.

"I have to see if she's truly not breathing. Sometimes these things can be temporary, you know. Perhaps even do CPR." She then straddled Taylor's dormant body.

"YOU? Do CPR?" scoffed James with a wry grin.

"What's wrong with that?" Camille remarked sharply.

"Well, that's an event in itself—don't you think?" he replied. "You don't know the first thing about it! That's like watching Liz Taylor become Mother Teresa!" he underscored. "What're you going to do? Give her your jewels for a prescription? Here Taylor, take three spoons of my liquid diamonds, a spoon full of gold will do, then remember to wash it down with my fabulous martini cocktail! You must be kidding me!" James derided. "What a joke!"
Camille was deeply insulted.

"You're the joker—YOU CLOWN!" she erupted. "Well, at least I don't ENJOY watching through the window, pretending I hated it— PEEPING TOM! So, who's the joker now, huh? IDIOT!"

Ferme la bouche, femme!" retaliated James in French. "Shut your mouth! You certifiable lunatic! Somebody ought to lock you up before you hurt yourself!" he hesitated. "BUT WAIT! They already DID!" he mocked, then roared in laughter.

"All right!" she shouted. "I've had it with you—JAMES THOMAS HUGHES! I want an apology right this minute!" she demanded.

"What? An apology?" he shook his head in amazement, then calmly moved closer to her and said. "Why don't you eat me? How's that for an apology?" He then smiled with smug satisfaction.

"That's it! You're leaving!" Camille threatened like her mother. "Out of this house and out of my life! I'm so tired of supporting your derrière and getting nothing in return! GET OUT NOW!" she screamed.

"YOU—kicking me out? Again?" James shot back. "What is it now, Camille—the fiftieth time?" He stared straight into her face, daring her. "You wouldn't last a second without me! I've been hearing you say that for the last twenty years. Christ! You're such a prima donna; you know that?"

Not one for diplomacy, the temperamental heiress gracefully headed over and struck him right between his eyes with her fist, putting an end to their strife once and for all. And down James went, hitting the floor with a terrific thud.

"That ought to teach you how to shut up!" she admonished.

Amanda was petrified. She was shocked that the two classiest people she had ever met could behave so primitively. Camille calmly returned to Taylor, reassessing her situation one last time. She tried to jiggle her body—it didn't move. She slowly turned her head to the side. Nothing. As a last-ditch effort, she leaned over Taylor's face, trying to feel her breath. Suddenly, Taylor convulsed back to life, and all three screamed at the top of their lungs, shocked beyond belief.

Camille lost control. Panicking like a mad woman, Camille took a heavy marble antiquity from the center table and nervously dropped it straight onto Taylor's head with such force that it gruesomely squashed her like a small bug. One eye popped out of the socket, and her fractured skull spilled parts of her brain on the floor. There laid Taylor's motionless body like a newly born lifeless chick. Everyone stood aghast as Amanda watched in horror. A carnage so shocking, it was an absolutely horrendous scene. "Oh, Cami..." James whispered, his eyes affixed to the dead teen.

"It was an accident..." she reasoned absently.

Complete silence filled the chateau.

* * *

The following day, Camille took one of her classic roadsters for a spin. A darkly tinted black "Lamborghini Diablo" with a contrasting yellow interior zipped in and around Monte Carlo. Locals and tourists alike were riveted by the gleaming car. Driving passed the Palace of Monaco; she entered the famous Princess Grace Avenue at the heart of Monte Carlo as she listened to her favorite rock band blasting through her car stereo. She slowed down to an intersection, eventually coming to a full stop, then turned her music down. Seconds later, a rental car with loud hip-hop music pulled up to her driver's side, filled with unruly teens. They, too, waited for the light to turn green. A cocky teenager at the passenger's side then rolled his window down, signaling Camille to do the same. The minute she did, the boys instantly let out a clamoring sound as if they were greatly disappointed.

"Excusez-moi, madam!" explained the teenager. "My friends and I made a bet that we could've sworn it had to be a man driving this gorgeous car of yours! And NOT a beautiful woman like you!" he chuckled. "I just lost that bet! But boy—aren't we ever glad to see you!"

Then grinning ear to ear lazily, he practically salivated to the point of embarrassment. As the boys awaited a reaction, Camille looked on but offered no response. She then took off her Chanel sunglasses, took a puff of her lit cigarette, and coolly blew smoke in their general direction. Still maintaining her composure, she turned to them and said, "idiots..." Then instantly pressing her foot at the gas pedal, Camille screeched off, leaving the boys in the dust.

Ten minutes later, she pulled up to the valet circle within the famous Square Beaumarchais—a prestigious collection of hotels, casinos, and upscale restaurants with Belle Epoque-style dining terraces—packed with tourists from all over the world. Camille preferred dining at Alain Ducasse's Le Louis XV three-star Michelin restaurant when frequenting an array of luxurious boutiques and romantic spots with a convivial atmosphere. Camille scoured top designer boutiques from Chanel to Christian Dior in search of the perfect evening gown. From there, she breezed through a chain of jewelry designers—including Van Cleef & Arpels, Chopard, Piaget, and Cartier—where she spotted a one-of-a-kind diamond-studded watch that she could not resist, a unique piece priced at three million that took various artists several months to finish.

"Bonjour, Mlle Rogers!" greeted a female sales associate, pleasantly surprised to see her V.I.P. client. "Nous ne savions pas que vous étiez en ville!"

"Bonjour! Comment tout le monde fait?" she answered, asking how everyone was doing.

"Très bonne Mlle Rogers" the woman replied.

Camille was instantly whisked to a private upstairs room designed for ultra-wealthy clientele like herself. A cold bottle of vintage champagne was opened and gracefully poured into an elegant flute served on a silver tray. Servers in uniform began to pass butler-style amuse-bouche, to canapés hors d'oeuvres such as: vol-au-vent, gougeres, garden pea and mint lollypop and toasted bellinis dolloped with saumon fumé, caviar and crème de marron.

Like Cinderella's famous glass slipper, the heavenly watch was a perfect match for Camille's beautiful wrist.

"N'est-ce pas chéri?" Camille reaffirmed.

Everyone in the room agreed.

"Shall I charge it to your house account, mlle?" asked the woman.
"Sûr...pourquoi pas?" Camille agreed on a whim.

The diamond jewelry watch was then wrapped in classic white paper and placed inside a signature red box. Camille left the store moments later with a medium-size red bag bearing the name Cartier printed in gold foil.

CARTER

Washington, DC ~ Beverly Hills ~ Hollywood: 1979 – 1999

12

Detective Evan Carter was ready to take his investigation to the next level. A local celebrity in the Beverly Hills Police Department, Carter believed that John Doe was the work of the elusive serial killer. Born and raised on the west side of Los Angeles, Carter, the only child of small business owners in Malibu, California, who surfed mostly in his earlier days, had a toughness about him. As a teenager, Carter's golden blond hair landed minor roles in films that earned him enough money to attend college. His parents provided the support and guidance he needed early on. Although they imposed limited structure or demands, Carter dreamt of joining the law enforcement community. He believed that good people like his parents must be protected and bad guys put away.

* * *

One morning, Carter received a call from a Washington D.C. area code.

"Detective Evan Carter?" Carlton asked in a courteous tone.

"Yes, this is Detective Evan Carter," he answered. "What can I do for you?" Carlton continued. "This is Special Agent Carlton from the Bureau."

"How can I help?"

"I was wondering if I could speak with you regarding the John Doe that your guys unearthed in the Beverly Hills Canyon area?" Carlton added. "I was hoping you could tell me more about him."

"Sure," Carter replied willingly. "How much time you got?"

"That's the thing, Detective—" Carlton sighed. "I really don't have a lot. I'm heading to San Francisco for a few days. I'd appreciate it if you could..."

"You got a case in Frisco?" interrupted Carter. "Why don't you stop by even for the day? It can't hurt."

Carlton hesitated. "No, I suppose not."

"I tell you what. You come here, and I will not only show you the body, but I will share more about our crime lab information," Carter informed him. "How's that? Anyway, your choice..."

"I would like that, Detective," Carlton replied. "How about if I check back with you next week?"

"Fine by me."

"I'll keep you posted once I have my schedule in front of me, all right? Thanks a lot."

"Don't mention it."

Five days later, Agent Carlton was on his way to see Detective Carter.

* * *

At around eleven o'clock in the morning, Carlton jumped out of a taxicab, grabbing his garment bag. He entered the crowded Dulles International Airport in Washington, D.C. Jostling through the crowd; he dreaded the check-in process. Carlton was not a fan of flying. He would put off projects that required travel and refused to travel by air whenever possible. He stressed out over trivial travel requirements and was agitated no matter how short his flight was. He simply despised traveling by plane.

After boarding the plane, he ordered a glass of Jack Daniels whiskey, neat. He looked out the window, cheerless and lost in thought. Hours later, he fought his way through the crowded Los Angeles International Airport. Renting a car, he headed to the three-star Hyatt hotel on Sunset Boulevard in West Hollywood. He checked in, took a quick shower, and put on a robe. He then dialed up Detective Carter, leaving a message announcing his late arrival.

* * *

The next morning, hours before his scheduled meeting with the detective, Carlton drove to the Beverly Hills Canyon area. Much to his surprise, yellow tape blocked his way. Another crime scene was in progress. Suddenly, a tow truck dragging a totaled police car swerved in front of him, halting behind an overturned garbage truck. Carlton stopped short, gazing at the crushed police car. Nodding to the officer-on-duty, he flashed his FBI badge from his window.

"Morning, officer," greeted Carlton. "What's going on here?"

"Morning..." the officer acknowledged while quickly scanning through his badge, then added. "I really don't know yet, sir. It happened just a few minutes ago."

"That fresh, huh?"

"Yup, they're on it right now," the officer replied. "An officer was shot, and his car plowed through the garbage truck." He glanced back at the scene. "It seems to me a mysterious death for now."

"You mean an accident?' replied Carlton.

"No, sir. I mean, there's a gunshot wound to the officer's right temple, but no fingerprints on the gun found at the scene," explained the officer.

"A hit squad taking down police officers?" Carter questioned. "Hopefully not, sir."

"Well...see you," Carlton said and drove on.

* * *

A short while later, he arrived at the Beverly Hills Police Department.

"Can I help you?" a female cop at the front desk asked.

"I'm here for Detective Carter?" Carlton said. "My name is Special Agent Carlton from the Bureau."

"It'll be just a minute, please."

"I'll wait."

Further down the hallway, Carter was tied up on a telephone call while trying to down a cold burger; Lieutenant Drake Monroe knocked softly on his door.

"I'll make sure of that," Carter said reassuringly on the telephone. "And yes, that's right, don't you worry about it, all right? I'll be in touch once I hear anything. Uh-huh..." He then spotted Monroe standing by the door and beckoned for him to enter.

"I'm sorry, Mrs. Thorsten, could I put you on hold for a minute?" he asked. "Just a quick minute, please. Thanks." He covered his speaker with one hand, turned to Monroe, and asked. "What is it, Lieutenant?"

"Special Agent Carlton is here to see you," said Monroe.

"Carlton, Carlton...where'd I know him from?" he pondered for a moment.

"He says he's from the FBI?"

"Oh yes! Great!" Carter said aloud. "Let him in, Lieutenant."

Minutes later, Carlton was ushered by Monroe into Carter's office. As they walked through the hallway, Carter wrapped up his call.

"You can wait here," Monroe instructed. "He'll be done in a minute. "Hope he's in a good mood."

"Good mood?" Carlton echoed.

"Special Agent Carlton!" Carter said, extending his hand, "Good to meet you!"

"I'd like to get right to it," said Carlton after the required pleasantries. He pulled out a notebook.

"Let's do it."

Then came another knock at the door.

"Got a minute, detective?" asked Monroe again. "You've got to see this. It's a thing of beauty."

"What?" the irascible detective snapped. "What is it now, Lieutenant— my lucky day?"

"More than that detective—if you can believe it," Monroe replied. He didn't take Carter's temper personally.

"All right, lieutenant, I'm coming," he hesitated. Monroe left, then popped his head back in seconds later. "And hey, could you get those weasels at the LA Coroners off my back? They've been calling like crazy."

"Yeah, yeah. Get out of here," Carter said, then grumbled to himself. "This better be worth my time." He faced Carlton and said. "Will you excuse me for a minute, Agent Carlton? Duty calls."

"Sure, sure. Whatever, man."

* * *

Ten minutes later, Carter returned to the office and swiftly put on his jacket.

"I'm sorry, Agent Carlton but something important has come up," he divulged. "I'm afraid we'll have to pick this up tomorrow." Quickly turning to Monroe, he blurted. "Lieutenant, would you give Mrs. Thorsten a call and see if we could come by in say about—" he glanced down to his watch. "Say about half an hour from now?" he added.

"You got it, detective," complied the lieutenant. "Nice meeting you, Agent Carlton, and uh, watch out for that man!" he jested, pointing to Carter as he left the room.

"Everything, all right?" Carlton asked Carter.

"Just bad timing. By the way, are you doing anything tonight?"

"No. Why?"

"I'm meeting a couple of friends at the Tavern bar at six," he said. "It's off of Sunset and Highland in West Hollywood. Decent food, nice music, but quiet. Why don't you meet me there for a drink around seven? We can talk more about the case."

Carlton hesitated for a moment, then accepted his invitation. "I can use a night out these days. Thanks, detective!"

"Great! See you then, Sherlock."

* * *

Carlton scanned the bar, saw the detective chatting with the bartender, and joined him. "It's nice to be off-duty every now and then," he told Carter. He ordered and quickly downed several shots of Jack Daniels.

"Hey, don't take this the wrong way," said Carter, "but I think you should go easy on those Jacks."

Carlton reacted sharply. "You sound like my wife, detective. That bitch is always on my case! Speaking of whom, I forgot. It's time to call the dragon lady."

"I thought you hated her," commented Carter.

Carlton smiled back. He headed to the front entrance, walked to the parking lot, lit up a cigarette, and dialed his wife from his cell phone. Moments later, the two were arguing again.

"Would you please shut your big mouth for one second?" he asked vehemently. "Maureen, this is not the reason I called! Put her on—now!" he shouted, then lowered his voice the next second. "Hey, sweetie. How's my angel?" he said gently, then listened in for a moment. "What?" he reacted. "Why didn't your mother call me? I'm so sorry, baby. I really am. But I'll be back home soon—OK? I love you, and things will be fine, I promise. OK, honey? Bye." He then heard a click on the other line.

Holding back swelling tears, Carlton composed himself before heading back in. He was never comfortable sharing his feelings with anyone, let alone a professional colleague. Minutes later, he was back inside the bar downing another shot of Jack Daniels.

"You all right, Carlton?" Carter asked.

"Yeah, yeah. I'm fine," he brushed him off. "Why don't we, um, call it a night, detective? I'm getting a little tired." He added. "Do you mind dropping me off a few blocks from here? I'll come back for my car first thing tomorrow morning."

"I'd be happy to."

"I appreciate that."

As Carter attempted to pay their bill, Carlton grabbed hold of the check. "No-no, I got this one," he insisted.

"Thanks, man."

Carlton took out his wallet and left plenty of cash on the counter.

CAMILLE AND JAMES

Monte Carlo ~ Cap d'Antibes ~ Canne: 1999

13

The next two weeks flew by. Camille's house servants packed a wardrobe for her upcoming trip with James. They carefully folded her haute couture gowns, designer hats, and accessories into Louis Vuitton travel luggage with golden brass corners. James packed tuxedos, suits, ties, and appropriate casual wear. They both looked forward to the trip. The European tour was part of L'Allure's annual unveiling of its latest collection, scheduled to begin at the "Cannes Film Festival" in Nice and moved on to Paris, London, Geneva, and Rome.

Seated at the back of a black vintage Corsica Bentley driven by a chauffeur, Camille spoke with her company's CEO about projects, yearly sales, contracts, and other business affairs. Twenty minutes later, the limousine entered the Monaco Heliport in Monte Carlo, pulling up to a luxurious private jet. The chauffeur rushed to open Camille's door, and out she came looking glamorous, followed by James wearing a dashing tailor-made jacket. Two bellhops sprung to assist, rolling out gold carts to fetch their luggage from the trunk.

The luxurious jet featured a customized double bed and a marble bathroom. Gold and crystal accents imitated diamonds throughout the aircraft. Custom-made leather seats were embossed with the letter "R." A spacious lounge decorated with velvet throw pillows filled the middle of the plane. The staff included a three-star Michelin chef, a first-class mixologist, a renowned Swedish masseur, and an award-winning pianist. For Camille, the jet was heaven.

Two pilots and a bevy of flight attendants in crisp royal blue uniforms stood at the door. Toasting one another with a French martini cocktail, Camille and James relaxed side by side in their seats. But a moment later, Camille discovered that one of her teardrop diamond earrings was missing. The set—estimated at ten million dollars—was gifted to her mother by Queen Victoria of England. Camille simply could "not afford" to lose part of this precious set.

"James darling..." she said, searching the pillows. "Have you seen my earring?"

James grinned as he took a sip of his martini. He then pointed to her drink without uttering a word. Camille quickly turned to her glass and saw a single teardrop earring gleaming at the bottom of her cocktail.

"Well, what do you know, darling," she smiled pleasantly. "A diamond in my cocktail!"

The two laughed cheerily. Camille took a deep breath. Feeling the tension drain from her body, she began to relax once again.

A short time later, the attendants brought out a bottle of their best champagne served in cold flute glasses, along with a tray of the world's most expensive caviar served on ice inside a twenty-four karat gold tin, paired with a plate of the finest European cheeses. The "Almas Iranian" caviar or better known as the "Royal caviar," had a rich and silky texture that melted in the mouth. Once named the most expensive food in the world, it cost a staggering thirty thousand dollars per can. Camille and James demanded royal treatment at thirty-nine thousand feet.

They soon landed at a private airport in Nice, met by another chauffeur, and traveled through historical landmarks of the Cap D'Antibes peninsula with breathtaking scenery. The stately gate of the timeless Hotel du Cap swung open, and the two entered the glamorous property. The former private mansion that captured the style and elegance of the French Riviera had been a legendary sanctuary for the rich and famous for nearly a century.

A handful of doormen welcomed their VIP guests at the valet entrance. Camille and James were quietly whisked through the lobby by the management, straight to their eight-bedroom private villa, avoiding the traditional check-in for regular guests. Moments later, the two were relaxing on their private patio under the scintillating sun with martinis in their hands, viewing an enormous private park with a secluded garden that showed Golden Age of Hollywood classic films at night and a magnificent infinity pool surrounded by the Mediterranean Sea. Life for the two could not have been more heavenly.

* * *

Lunching in the hotel's finest dining room the next day, Camille and James took in the beautiful sea view through floor-to-ceiling windows. A waiter wearing a white jacket and a black tie placed two martini cocktails on the table.

"Bonne après-midi, Mlle Rogers!" the friendly waiter greeted them. "Welcome back!" Then he turned to James, asking how he was doing. "Comment vas-tu, Monsieur James?"

"Tout est bien," James replied.

"Bonjour, mon bon ami! Well, aren't you a doll?" Camille said jubilantly to the waiter, then added. "Darling, please bring me a César Salade from the gourmet buffet in the other room. I'm afraid I overdid it at the party last night..." she hinted, winking at him.

"Pas de problème mademoiselle," the dreamy-eyed waiter happily complied. "Awww...merci beaucoup."

Camille rose up to use the powder room. James immediately stood up, showing proper etiquette.

"I shall return, darling," she announced, then gracefully exited the floor.

James sat back down, then turned to the waiter to resume his order. "You know what, my friend? I'd like to have what she's having, s'il vous plaît," he said. But the waiter stood perplexed.

"Monsieur!" The apoplectic waiter chided with a distinct French accent. "How could you ask me for a César Salade when you have... perfectly DEUX good legs and DEUX good arms? Mon Dieu!" he excoriated, his face turning red. "This restaurant monsieur por ton information...happens to serve the finest gourmet buffet including

111

César Salade! And if you want to have your César Salade—I suggest you get it yourself!" Then he turned around and walked away like a temperamental fool.

James was rendered speechless, dumbstruck by what he heard. Moments later, he noticed the same waiter gathering ingredients for a César Salade dish from the elegant buffet, which he then carried joyously on a silver platter and served to Camille. James was in shock. He looked at Camille, who winked back at him with a charming smile.

Two days later, an evening of glitz and glamour engulfed the beautiful town of Cannes in Nice. The Annual Cannes Film Festival drew huge crowds from all over the world. Hollywood moguls and stars flaunted their expensive attire and jewelry. Royalties, aristocrats, socialites, and dignitaries attended movie premieres, while others debuted their films, parading on red carpets for worldwide coverage and publicity. Camille and James were there to promote their film and their latest jewelry line. The event also provided an opportunity to reconnect with old acquaintances and to make new contacts.

Camille's attention-grabbing ensemble was absolutely ravishing. James, with his debonair looks, was equally impressive in a cream and black lapel tuxedo. Against a backdrop of flashing lights and howling fans, the paparazzi took special interest in Camille's astonishingly large teardrop diamond necklace.

"Mlle Rogers! Over here!" one photographer shouted.

"Right here, Camille!" his colleague repeated.

"Mlle Rogers! Can you tell us about your mother's movie?" a third one asked. "I hear there are A-list movie stars in it?"

James and Camille suddenly found themselves in a pool of hungry vultures. Easy targets for fashion and jewelry magazine front covers, the attractive pair and their "movie star looks" were among the most talked about in Hollywood circles. Moments later, the two successfully escaped the madness outside and made it to the lobby adjoining the auditorium.

"Can you believe these guys?" Camille remarked, primping herself on the wall mirror.

"Well, that's what happens when someone as beautiful as you wears a phenomenal piece, my love," James complimented.

Camille was flattered. "Why, thank you, darling!" she smiled, then held up her necklace's centerpiece, gazing steadily at the jewel in the mirror. "Yes, quite a stunning piece," she said softly. Flashbacks of vivid childhood memories came rushing back.

At four years of age, Camille was blindfolded by her mother and taken to her private jewelry collection for the first time. Camille opened her eyes to gleaming strands of crystals dripping down in various shapes and sizes. Camille was stunned by the treasure trove of sparkling jewelry, a lifetime memory for the young heiress.

"Shall we, mon chéri?" asked James.

Camille snapped out of her reverie. "But of course, darling!" she smiled. Entering the auditorium, the two wove through the crowd to their VIP seats in the front row. Seconds passed. The room darkened, and the crowd fell silent. The first movie began to roll.

* * *

Several hours later, James and Camille attended an exclusive party for celebrities, royalty, and aristocrats in the Grand Ballroom. They remained in their seats as movie stars, and socialites stopped by to greet them.

A dark hair green-eyed handsome stranger sat a few tables away. The mid-forties heir to the Ferrari sports car brand had been eyeing Camille all evening. Keenly aware of his interest, Camille pretended not to see him. She whispered to James, then left the room. All eyes trailed her as she departed. A short time later, James joined Camille in the front lobby.

"Well, that was bizarre..." Camille commented, puffing away on a cigarette. "I just chatted with Aunt Laura...remember her? I never thought I'd see that woman again." "Wait!" James lit up. "THE aunt Laura? Your mother's friend from down the road where we picked berries and got bitten by her dog? Well, I did but not you."

"That's her. Shocking, isn't it?" Camille replied. "Darling, what do you think of cutting out soon?"

At that exact moment, the handsome stranger stood in front of her.

"Hello there..." he greeted flirtatiously in a deeply Italian accent.

James glanced at Camille, still as a mouse.

"My name is Lorenzo Ferrari," he introduced. "Perhaps you have heard of me. I am the grandson of Enzo Ferrari, the car Ferrari and—"

"And how unfortunate," Camille cut in, then blew smoke in his face.

Camille was not at all impressed with the Italian stud. Fresh and ungentlemanly, his presumptuous demeanor was in poor taste. To approach her so cavalierly and expect her to fall for him—all in the name of "Ferrari"—was a cardinal sin in her book. Not that she entertained the thought of dating the legions of wealthy and viable suitors chasing after her, from Earls to Dukes, movie stars and now the heir to a sports car conglomerate. Camille loathed bad manners. She did not suffer fools gladly, and James knew her idiosyncrasies all too well.

"You look like you could be a movie star," the cocky stranger continued. "So, what do you think of the best actress?"

Camille studied him for a moment and continued puffing away.

"Well..." she remarked calmly. "I thought her bosom was rather large," then hesitated. "Hmm...I wonder what might happen if she takes off her brassiere?" Ruminating for a second, she looked at him and added. "Perhaps her cows might come home?" She turned and walked away.

"WHOA!" said James. An awkward moment passed between the two men. James was embarrassed; the Ferrari heir was visibly befuddled. His date for the night, a buxom blonde, suddenly appeared from behind.

"Oh, there you are!" she said animatedly. "I knew I'd find you here!"

Camille winked at him from a distance. Sighing regretfully, he turned to his date and gave her a faint smile.

"You have a good evening, sir," James said with forced gaiety.

"You...too," he replied absently, still processing what had just occurred.

James rushed to catch up with Camille in the valet parking area. Surprised by her behavior, he could not hold back. "Camille! People do not appreciate it when you say things like that!" he blurted out.

"I know! How scandalous!" she said dismissively with a fiendish smile, adding, "Who cares, darling!"

Camille then walked ahead of him and slipped into the waiting limousine.

BRAD

Èze Village ~ Monte Carlo: 1982 – 1999

14

On a late Saturday afternoon, James raced around in his black polished Ducati 916 motorcycle with a matching helmet, cruising the charming town of Èze Village. His morning was filled with personal errands for Camille, and he was now feeling ravenous. He slowed down as he neared a café, stopping for a coffee and fresh pastry. He was locking up his bike with a metal chain when a young man approached him.

Brad Müller, a seventeen-year-old exchange student from Germany with deep blue eyes and a movie fanatic, was on summer holiday.

"This is what we call a thing of beauty!" the vibrant teen praised in a German accent. "She is gorgeous!"

"Thanks, bud," James said. "Yes, she's a doll, isn't she?"

"More than a doll, my friend! I'd say I'll take her straight home! Wham, bam, thank you, ma'am!" he jested, laughing it off.

"You'd be surprised how comfortable she is too," James revealed and added, "I know I was."

"No kidding?"

"Nope."

Brad then moved closer to the motorbike though he sought his approval first. "May I?" he asked politely.

"Be my guest," James replied. "I have to grab my coffee, and I'll be right back, OK? Enjoy yourself!"

James then walked away.

"Whatever, man! I'll be here," he responded inattentively.

When James returned, he saw Brad still admiring his motorbike. He immediately halted and hid around the corner, discreetly observing for him a moment. Then he walked back again.

"So, you like her that much, huh?" asked James.

The curious teen was enthralled. "verdammt!," he replied then quickly apologized. "Oh, I'm sorry, man. When I get excited, I start speaking German!" he explained. "Anyway, you kidding? I've always wanted to have one like this! I mean, look at it, the very, very bad things I can do to this baby! Gott hilf mir!, he teased. Bestimmt!," James reciprocated.

Brad hesitated for a second. "Right on, my man!" he chuckled, impressed with his German fluency.

But James was hatching a plan. "Um, if you really like this bike, we have a collection at home not far from here," James revealed. "Would you like to see it?"

Brad's eyes burst with excitement. "Really, man? That's very kind of you!" He then introduced himself. "By the way, I'm Brad..."

Both men exchanged handshakes.

"I'm James—James Hughes," he replied. "Come to think of it; we have a beauty parked in our yacht. If you don't mind, we'll stop there. It's closer than our house—about seven minutes away."

"Oh, I thought you were going to say, 'the name is Hughes—James Hughes,'" Brad said. "You know like the name is Bond, James Bond. You kind of look like him, anyway."

James smiled back.

"Wait a minute!" Brad halted and added. "Did you just say you have a yacht?"

"I did."

"You mean, one of those big things out there?"

"Not the biggest, but big enough," countered James. "But yes, one of those big things out there. It belongs to my family," he continued. "So, come on! Hop on! I'll give you a ride! Where were you heading anyway?"

"Wherever you're going, man!" Brad exalted.

He climbed onto James' motorcycle, and the two drove away as the sun began to set. They arrived at the loading dock of the Monaco Harbor minutes later. Yachts of all sizes spilled out of their designated water parking spaces, many hosting romantic parties, and rowdy gatherings. He had not been exposed to so much wealth during his young life. Minutes passed.

James and Brad reached a very large boat covered in a unique design: a black-and-white tuxedo with diamond-like buttons stood out in the harbor. The two entered the lavish interior. Sitting comfortably on the living room couch, Camille was reading her glossy jewelry magazine called Piaget.

"WHOA!" he reacted, overwhelmed by the surrounding luxury. "Some yacht you got here!" he marveled. "You guys must be filthy rich!" Then added. "I mean, money to burn RICH!"

He then noticed Camille in a corner.

"Oh excusez-moi mlle," he said humbly in French, embarrassed.

Camille and James glanced at each other, then laughed it off.

"Glad you like it, my friend!" said James. "Brad, I'd like you to meet Camille." He turned to her and continued. "Camille, Brad, I uh, was going to show him my new bike?"

"Oh, what fun! Bonjour." Camille reacted. "An unexpected guest. James darling..." "Yes, mon chéri?"

"Why don't you show Brad your latest achievement?"

"Good idea!" James agreed. "Thanks for reminding me."

"I'm certain he will be fascinated by it." Camille smiled, then winked at Brad. "You boys have fun!"

"Come, Brad, I'll show you my latest," said James.

Glancing back at Camille as he walked away, Brad said, "Nice to meet you!" "Également!" Camille replied.

James and Brad continued talking as they walked through the boat corridor. "So, I built this cool room for gaming," James began. "with the latest high-tech gadgets. It's on the same level where I keep my bike, but we don't have to go if—" "Are you kidding, man?" Brad interrupted. "No, I can't wait! Sounds like an awesome project!"

"Want to have a drink first?"

"No! Drinks come after!"

"You're the boss!" James smiled, motioning him forward. "Well then, walk this way, young man!"

"When did you finish the room?"

"Not long ago. Maybe about a month or so ago..."

"Cool."

The unsuspecting teen trailed behind James down the basement to a narrowing hallway, eventually coming to a full stop. A stainless steel door stood before them.

"Well, there it is!" James presented. "Go ahead, check it out!"

"Don't mind if I do!" Brad said, dashing inside a dungeon-like room with several steel bars.

"This is so unbelievable!" the teenager reacted fervently, then looked around. "I wish I had something like this back at home. It's gorgeous, man!" he hesitated. "Wait! This cell reminds me of something—"

"Dr. Hannibal Lecter in Silence of the Lambs, I hope?" reminded James.

"I knew it! DAMN!" Brad replied gleefully. "It sure feels like one, too! I've seen that movie thirty times, you know. I love that movie!"

"Smart young man."

Brad zeroed in his interest back to the cell.

"Well, what're you waiting for?" Brad smiled. "Lock me in, dude! I want to see what it feels like to live inside like Dr. Lector!"

"You said it..." James said nonchalantly.

James pushed the remote control, immediately closing the door. It reached from one wall to the other, locking up Brad. CLICK.

"Man, I can't wait 'til my brother gets a load of this!" Brad continued. "His friends will dig this baby, for sure! This is so amazing, my friend!" Then putting on a serious face, he looked at James and said in a sobering tone. "You really ought to start locking up real people," he then loosened up. "You know, try them for size!"

"I did," James replied.

"What do you mean you did?" the teen asked nervously. "Come on, man...this isn't funny," he insisted. "Come on, let me out!"

"You said to lock up real people. You couldn't be more real to me," responded James with an impassive voice. "Congratulations, young man. You're officially my first capture," he divulged.

"What did you say?" Brad asserted, still puzzled by the exercise. Slowly sinking back to reality, he exclaimed. "You have got to be kidding me! You can't do this to me! Come on, buddy!" he pleaded. "Come on— OPEN UP!"

James continued to ignore the teen.

"I was only kidding—YOU FREAK!" Brad shouted his frustrations. "Listen, let me out! NOW! I'm going to tell your friend Camille!"

James chuckled, shaking his head.

"Camille," he mocked, shaking his head. "That's right; she'll help you. Whatever, man."

He was gone the next minute.

* * *

At one o'clock in the morning, James was back at the Chateau. Amanda, taped and bound, was kicking and screaming to no avail. A burlap sack covered her head. Fearing that the weekend housemaids would discover her, James decided to transfer her to the yacht. He dragged the uncooperative mother from the basement, pushed and shoved her into the kitchen, across the living room, and into the elevator down to their subterranean garage. He placed her in the trunk of a discreet car and drove back to the Monaco Harbor.

The drive took him about twenty minutes though it felt much longer. He continued to block racing thoughts. The coast was clear at the loading dock. He took Amanda out of the trunk and led her to the yacht, discreetly sticking a black eight-inch hunting knife in her back as he kept an eye out for a potential witness. Once inside, he placed her in front of the fireplace in the living room, made a beeline for the steering room, turned on the engine, and pulled away from the dock. The elegant yacht gracefully moved out to sea.

A short time later, James shut the engine and dropped an anchor in the water. The beautiful horizon of a distant glistening Monte Carlo took his breath away—as if heaven had just parted its gates. James took a long and deep breath. All his fears, worries, and anxieties suddenly melted away. Minutes later, he returned to the living room.

"Here you go, sweetie," he said, pulling the bag over her head. "Now, we're going to have fun! I'll be right back, OK?" He quickly turned around and disappeared.

He returned with Brad minutes later, also taped and bound with shackles on both his hands and feet. He placed him next to Amanda.

"There you go!" James said. "Now the two of you can finally get acquainted—isn't this much better?" he smiled. "Brad, meet Amanda. Amanda, Brad. What a perfect match! Camille has got to see this!"

Instantly, the two complained in muffled voices. But the lights dimmed, and suddenly the room was black. Trumpets blared, and the lights gradually returned. All of a sudden, Camille popped out of a corner with a huge spotlight following her across the living room—utterly flawless.

She took over the room portraying Rita Hayworth playing Gilda singing "Put the Blame on Mame."

"When they had the earthquake in San Francisco back in 1906..." she began to sing away. "That's the story that went around, but here's the real low down. Put the blame on mame, boys, put the blame on mame.

"What-the?" James whispered absently.

Brad and Amanda were astonished. James loved the show. He jumped on the piano and began to play and sing, harmonizing with Camille like a famous duo. Before long, the two were living in their own world. James, dazzled by the performance, threw praise and chants from across the room, clapping, howling, and whistling with adulation.

"Well done, my love!" he commended. "You are the single greatest star anyone could ever wish for! Aren't they lucky to have seen your talent? WELL DONE, MY LOVE! WELL DONE!" he shouted.

Turning to Brad and Amanda next, he said, "OK guys, she's coming!" he warned. "I want you to stand up! STAND UP for God's sake!" he demanded. "Now, this is your chance to thank Camille for the amazing performance she's given us, OK? "Oh, one more thing—don't ask for her autograph just yet." He then continued. "Cause she won't like that! OK? All good? We're set? LET'S DO IT!"

Brad and Amanda looked at each other and quickly realized they were in the presence of a deranged couple—TOTAL MANIACS. Shocked and bewildered, they devolved to becoming defiant the next minute. If looks could kill, James and Camille would have already been dead.

"Oh, I forgot!" James suddenly remembered. "You guys can't talk this way, can you now?" he reasoned. "How insensitive of me." He stripped the tape off their mouths.

Camille, smoking coolly, quietly observed the scene. Then Brad let out his frustrations, unleashing his fury.

"OUCH! YOU CRAZY LUNATICS!" the boy ranted. "You will pay for this! You kidnapped us! Held us captive!" he shouted. "I'm going to report you both to the Monaco Police! I hate you two! I hate you!"

But Camille remained unfazed, cool as a cucumber. Again she simulated Rita Hayworth in another memorable scene.

Moving like a Cheshire cat, she gracefully moved closer to Brad and whispered in his ear. "Hate is a very exciting emotion—haven't you noticed?" she began. "Very exciting—I hate you too, Johnny boy," she continued. "I hate you so much that—I think I'm going to die from it, darling." Then laughed maniacally as she walked away, astonishing everyone.

James glanced at the two for a moment, then roared with Camille in laughter. Repulsed by what he witnessed, Brad shook his head in disbelief.

"You guys make me sick!" he moaned.

Late that evening—with Brad and Amanda slumped over and fast asleep on the living room couch—James and Camille opted for a good night's sleep. James decided to retape Brad's mouth when the angry teen—pretending to be asleep—suddenly bit his hand, causing it to bleed.

"JEEE—SUS! You cannibal piece-of-shit!" exclaimed James checking his hand. "You bit me, you fool! Now look what you did—I'm bleeding! HAPPY NOW?"

Brad grinned with a smug look on his face. Amanda slowly awoke.

"I thought you liked that kind of stuff!" Brad said in retaliation. "Now you know how I feel."

A brief moment went by. Camille heard a loud thump. With a clenched fist, James took a good swing at Brad from the backside, knocking him out cold. Brad instantly fell over, hitting his head on the floor. Amanda, fearing for her life, watched in disbelief.

"What the devil did you do that for, James?" Camille asked sharply. "It was all under control!"

"Yeah, well, he bit me!" countered James.

"And you slug him in return?" Camille replied. "What kind of man are you?"

"The kind who gives back what people deserve."

* * *

124

At one o'clock in the morning, a torrential downpour caromed off the yacht, bleeding into the night. Thunderstorms and lightning developed, quickly darkening the heavenly paradise of Monte Carlo. A shadowy figure wearing a dark cloak sat alone in the dining area of the boat—brooding in silence, mired in an internal struggle.

Slipping on an elegant, white masquerade ball mask with gold trimming, the fast-moving stranger rose up, headed to the lower level, and quietly stared at the captured teen.

Brad was lying face down, totally incapacitated. Awakening to a groggy feeling, he immediately felt sick when trying to twist around. He knew he had been drugged. Adjusting his vision, a foreboding figure came into view, standing before him.

"Hey . . .what's going on?" he asked imploringly.

A long silence followed. The figure closed in on him and, without warning, jabbed a ten-inch dagger into his back.

"NO—NOOOO! AAAHHHH!" he screamed. "God please—NO!"

Blood spurted furiously. A fusillade of exactly twenty-one stab wounds went into his back, his neck, and onto his skull—tearing his skin apart. His lungs were punctured. The knife went in and out of his body. Brad fought desperately for his life, gasping each time the weapon penetrated.

Surprisingly, the killer stopped. As though part of a psychological game, the predator (or the consumer in this case) drove pleasure from watching his victims take their last breath. Similar to an Asian culture, where live fish was served on a "lazy Susan" as a delicacy, the predator was hailed as a "hero" for taking the fish's last breath. Brad mustered his last strength, painfully trying to force his words out.

"Stop—please," he pleaded.

But like a trained militant—vicious and ruthless—even to the end, the bloodthirsty assassin slit his throat for the finale. A rush of adrenaline, releasing like a powerful sedative, gave the killer the much-needed "fix." Minutes after, Brad's neck snapped off from the beheading, his head rolling to the side corner, with eyes wide open.

As a symbolic move, the killer closed his victim's eyes and vanished into the darkness.

DR. K

Eze Village ~ Beverly Hills: 1957 – 1999

15

It was a lazy Sunday. At half past noon, Camille and James basked under the sun of a Michelin-starred cliff-side patio restaurant, sipping on peach Bellini cocktails.

Chateau Eza, a former 16th-century Royal Palace in Eze Village at Côte d'Azur, radiated a world of medieval charm and beauty with old traditions. Fresh local ingredients, highly-skilled chefs, and impeccable service earned rave reviews, but a striking view of the breathtaking Mediterranean Sea below was their most coveted asset.

"Oh, good heavens!" Camille startled. "I've run out of cigarettes again!" She said to James. "I apologize, my darling—but would you be an angel and get some from the bar?"

"None at all, meh lady," James complied, teasing her with a British accent. He stood up and went inside the main house.

Camille was immediately mesmerized by two adorable children playing near the next table. A free-spirited five-year-old brunette in a princess tulle flower dress was trailed by her six-year-old brother, a blonde boy in a mini-tuxedo tailcoat. Reminded of her childhood, Camille recalled when James watched over her. Her mind wandered to a scene that occurred when she was thirteen. And yet she remembered it so well. It was a cold night. Pale and disheveled, Camille sat atop her bathroom toilet in her nightgown, sweating in pain. Clenching her teeth hard on a rolled hand towel, a baleful event was about to unfold. Claire, growing suspicious, tapped at the door.

"Camille, darling, is everything all right in there?" She asked curiously.

Camille, startled.

"I'm fine, mother!" she replied nervously. "I uh, just need a few more minutes... I'll be right out soon!" she assured her.

Hours later, Camille slipped out of the bathroom. Carrying a bundle wrapped in pink swaddling cloth in her arms, she gingerly walked the hallway—the stairwell—down to the lobby—across the living room—then out the patio garden. James stood waiting with a flashlight and a shovel—a shallow ground was dug. She carefully placed the "bundle" into the small dent in the earth. A poignant reminder of how precious life could be, Camille welled up in tears. James then shoved some earth soil back into the ground.

"Stop!" Camille said firmly.

Bending down on her knees, she opened the sweater. The patio garden stood still. There laid her dead infant, cold as ice, with her eyes shut tight to the world. Specs of blood and blue veins marred her beautiful face. Camille tucked a light pink rose between the baby's tiny hands, pushing the rose to her chest as if the baby was praying. She closed the sweater, gazed at the infant, and sighed deeply. Baby Doe looked more like a "baby angel" sleeping peacefully. She was overwhelmed by a profound sense of grief and sadness.

Back at the bar, James was settling the bill when he heard a television announcement about two missing American tourists: Amanda and Taylor Collins. The US FBI promised a thorough investigation. Shaken, James scurried out the door, leaving his receipt on the counter.

* * *

Days later, James was in his private Chateau office, thumbing through a magazine. The office, a retro-room lifted from a 1940s film noir set, had see-through glass windows and wooden blind slats, with a wide sign above the front door that boldly proclaimed:

128

PRIVATE INVESTIGATOR

Rogers & Associates

Amanda, unbathed for days, was fast asleep. Crouching in a corner, she was cuffed on both wrists and her ankles and was chained to a pole. She opened her eyes and saw a doctor quietly working behind the desk. An older woman well in her 60s, with short salt-and-pepper hair, she was wearing a white lab jacket and thick black-rimmed glasses. Confused by her presence, Amanda startled, flinching backward.

"Who are you?" she asked suspiciously.

"Don't be alarmed, dear," the doctor said in a calm, washed-out European accent. "My name is Dr. K. I'm a colleague of Camille and James," she added. "I've worked with them for a long time—for more than ten years now."

Dr. K substituted for Camille and James in situations that required her special expertise. Educated both at Paris Descartes University and Harvard Medical School in the United States, Dr. K held two doctorate degrees in medicine and surgery. She was a sought-after hire in the medical field for many prestigious institutions, including the Rogers Foundation. The only scientist with a breakthrough formula that healed childhood cuts in a single day, her work was hailed as the next "Lorenzo's Oil" by many experts—healing the rarest of illnesses and diseases for children—and later dubbed as the "miracle ointment" by the press.

Although retired from the world stage, Dr. K never lost her passion for medicine. Now privately hired by wealthy families like Princess Diana of Wales and Camille Rogers, her clients shared her passion for saving children around the world. Trustworthy and experienced, Camille knew who to turn to when it came to advanced medical research.

"You must be hungry," Dr. K said to Amanda. "There are fresh tea sandwiches here—would you like some?" she offered.

"Yeah, I could use a few," answered Amanda.

Taking the elegantly plated tier stand with petit fours and savory tea sandwiches from her desk, Dr. K handed it over to Amanda.

"Here you go," she said.

"Thanks."

"There's a bottle of water next to you by the wall if you need it."

Amanda took one bite, and she was in heaven. Gorging down the rest, she devoured every piece while Dr. K opened a cabinet close by and grabbed small bottles.

"So, you're aware; I was assigned to your case to ensure you receive proper care and nutrition for your evaluation. I'm a psychiatrist," she revealed.

Amanda was flustered.

"A psychiatrist?" she asked. "Well, what's that got to do with me? Isn't that for CRAZY people?"

"Not necessarily," Dr. K replied casually. "BUT—there's always the exception."

"What exception?" questioned Amanda. "What the heck are you talking about?"

Dr. K was silent. Focused on her research, she picked up a medical book on her desk.

"Why are they doing this?" Amanda persisted.

"Doing what?" Dr. K responded.

"THIS! What else?" she exclaimed. "This weird thing that they are doing to me! Whatever the heck you, CRAZY people do—what do you think?" Lowering her voice, she added. "Speaking of strangeness…hey, what happened to that boy?"

Dr. K was genuinely puzzled. "I'm not sure who you're referring to Mrs. Collins," she answered.
Amanda suddenly remembered.

"Brad!" she said aloud. "His name is Brad! The German blonde boy whom they also took? Don't—you—know?" she asked quizzically.

"I'm afraid I can't answer that, Mrs. Collins," said the doctor. "I'm only here to do my duties, you see," she argued matter-of-factly. "Other than that, this process must be completed before they can actually let you go."

Deeply encouraged, Amanda's eyes lit up.

"Let me go? Are you serious?" she repeated. "They would do that?"

"Yes—of course," replied Dr. K. Then, looking Amanda straight in the eyes, she smiled. "They're not killers, Mrs. Collins. They know you're not the type who would turn on them," she continued. "They already feel indebted to you due to your daughter's accident. Trust me, if anybody felt bad about this, they do," she insisted. "Take my word for it."

Amanda let out a huge sigh of relief. Feeling the stiffness in her body abate, she began to relax.

"You see, Mrs. Collins my job here is to help you achieve that," Dr. K assured her. "Starting with this vitamin shot that I'm about to give you."

Straightaway, the medical expert jabbed a syringe in her arm when she was not looking.

"But…" she countered weakly.

Within seconds, Amanda blacked out.

* * *

Midnight struck. Amanda slept like a baby for the first time. Still, losing her daughter and witnessing another teen disappear was more than she could take. Her only hope now was a daring escape. But it would take guts. Minutes later, she was startled awake by a terrifying blast of light pointed at her face. A mysterious figure moved around in the darkness, taunting her with a flashlight, switching it on and off. Amanda felt she was under observation.

"Camille? James?" she asked nervously. "Who's there? What'd you want?"

But the stranger remained silent and soon vanished into the darkness.

* * *

Halfway across the world, days later, Camille and James were driven around Beverly Hills in their limousine following the Academy Awards ceremony. L'Allure's latest collection was showcased by dozens of movie stars on the red carpet.

A jewelry royalty known to the Hollywood elites, Camille was welcomed with warmth and respect. She was a celebrity in her own right. Power and influence placed her at the top of the most coveted dining reservation lists and VIP parties around town.

Pulling up to the valet, the limousine entered the driveway of an iconic pink building beaming with luxury. The white and green sign beautifully spelled out: Beverly Hills Hotel. Attendants lined up in advance for their arrival, and a white-gloved doorman reached out to open Camille's door. She stepped out, followed by James, and both entered the lobby.

A middle-aged French Maître d' from the Polo Lounge restaurant greeted them.

"Bonsoir, Mlle Rogers!" he said jubilantly, kissing Camille on both cheeks.

"Bonsoir, Pierre! Comment ça va?" replied Camille. "How's the family?"

"Oh, fine Mlle, just fine!" he answered. Turning to James next, he nodded. "Monsieur Hughes, good evening to you."

"Good evening, Pierre," greeted James.

"So good to see you both!" Pierre said. "I certainly hope LA has graced you with the same love and beauty as did French Riviera! So, tell me—how was the Oscar Awards?" he asked.

"Bored out of my mind, as usual, darling," Camille responded. "Nothing we haven't seen before." She then added. "I must have been doing this for far too long."

All three laughed simultaneously.

Minutes later, Pierre led them to Camille's favorite booth tucked in the corner. All eyes stared at the beautiful pair.

"You two have a lovely dinner," Pierre smiled.

"Merci beaucoup, Pierre," Camille reciprocated, then sent her best to his wife. "Envoyer mon meilleur à votre femme. À plus tard."

"It's very kind of you, Mlle Rogers. I will. Merci," Pierre replied, then left the room.

"Well, that was a colossal waste of an evening," Camille blurted, referring to the event. "BUT someone had to do it, right?" She picked up the menu and began to read it. "It's good for business, I suppose," she added.

"Put on a smile, frown when they turn," teased James.

"Easy now, darling. You know how much I 'like' people," Camille quipped.

A few tables away, an overweight country bumpkin walked in, seemingly lost. James looked up and saw the woman.

"You are never going to believe this, but look who's—come—ming," James announced quietly in a singsong way.

Camille turned to see. Her eyes followed intently as the languid woman walked past their table.

"Bee-utiful," she remarked dryly. Then quickly turning to James, she jested. "Give me a stick, and I'll kill it, darling!"

James burst into a loud guffaw. Attracting a little too much of the wrong attention, Camille quelled him with a look, and he quickly quieted down.

CARLTON

Washington, DC ~ Monaco: 1999

16

A barrage of criticism hit the FBI in Washington, D.C. The case of two missing American tourists—Amanda and Taylor—continued to dominate news headlines across the globe. Facing mounting pressure, Carlton and his special task force worked tirelessly. Everyone in his department was expected to perform their level best. The Collins investigation was now in full swing.

But the star agent hit dead ends from his leads, one after another. Desperate for answers, he had an epiphany one day. Hoping to break the case, he dialed up names from his European contact list in his office. First, he spoke with MI6 in London, then with Interpol and the Inspectors in France, and finally with the local authorities in Monaco. Moving on to the next call, a colleague suddenly popped his head in.

"Hey Carlton, the boss wants you in his office..." he babbled hurriedly.

"I'm in the middle of solving a case!" Carlton yelled out sharply. "That is if you guys don't mind."

"Time for you to take a breather," his colleague continued. "For the season that is."

Sensing trouble, Carlton put down his phone.

"What do you mean, take a breather?" he asked in a caustic voice.

"Don't look at me. I'm just the messenger," explained his colleague, then he left.

Internalizing for a moment, Carlton rose up and slammed his fists on his desk.

Collectively, his growing frustrations came crashing down. Striding through the hallways, his Italian blood boiling, he walked straight into his boss' office.

"So just like that—you cut me loose, huh?" he fumed.

A distinguished-looking retired four-star general, Carlton's boss entered a second career serving as the current FBI Director. Bored from his retirement in Florida, his love for the intelligence community kept him in the loop. He was in the middle of a meeting with agents when Carlton interrupted.

"Agent Carlton!" he said with a tinge of anger. Then he motioned the other agents to leave the room. "Sit down," he continued. "I presume this is about your time off?"

"No, it's about my beauty tips," Carlton remarked snidely. "Of course, being forced to leave—what do you think?" he added.

"Look, Carlton," the boss began in a sober tone. "I don't want to be the one to tell you this, but you've been slacking on a lot of fronts lately."

"That is just so ill-advised," muttered Carlton, shaking his head.

"And now with this new case," his boss continued. "Christ! I got everybody from the Mayor to the relatives of the missing mother and daughter going public, each holding their own press conferences, sometimes simultaneously!" he unloaded. "And God knows what they will do next! Not to mention, I received a call from the President this afternoon asking where the hell we are with this!" Then turning back to Carlton, he yelled, "And YOU—haven't got the slightest clue who dun it! So, do I think it's time for you to take a hike for now? I'd say yeah, think so!" He added. "Or should I mention your daughter?"

"HEY!" Carlton exploded with rage. "You don't get to talk about my daughter! EVER! You got that? And how would you know what leads I got since you are too busy playing politics and ridding me, huh?"

His boss backed down. "Look, Carlton," he softened. "I know this has been hard on you and your family. Why don't you take a vacation with your daughter? You can finally spend time with each other, for God's sake. Bring her to a place she really likes, and who knows; it might do you both good." Then he hesitated. "I can't even imagine if it were my own daughter."

"That's right!" Carlton cut in angrily. "YOU can't! So, let's just save all this bullshit for another time, huh? And stop pretending like you do know because you DON'T—OK?" he scowled, slamming the door behind him.

Hours later, Carlton was back at his local bar having shots of his favorite Jack Daniel's whiskey, escaping the turmoil he faced at work daily and the albatross that awaited him at home.

To Carlton, the taste of alcohol gave him a sense of "belonging" he did not find at work or at home. It calmed his nerves down and brought him comfort even though he knew it was only temporary. While the outside world crawled with pessimism and despair, he felt safe the moment he took that first sip. Another tragic homicide could break in at any minute, as history would inevitably repeat itself. Regardless, it was all worth it for Carlton.

Driving back home close to midnight, he pulled over at a busy Dulles International Airport runway. From a distance, he witnessed a Boeing 747 take off while another landed. His parents took him to the airport runway to watch the planes as a child. A perpetual symbol of beginning to end, first and last, and the Alpha and Omega—the sight had fascinated him since he was a young boy. Reflecting behind the cross-wire fence, he was haunted by his failures, indulgences, and fears.

* * *

The following Saturday early afternoon, Camille read a book in the salon while sipping at her afternoon tea, just like her mother. Classical tunes from the world's musical geniuses like Beethoven and Chopin were playing softly in the background.

Down in the basement, Amanda found a hairpin on the ground and immediately worked to remove her cuffs. Trembling and sweating, her cuffs snapped open minutes later. Amanda sprang into action. She ransacked the place, sifting every drawer, looking for keys.

A beautiful antique French armoire stood out, with a rustic padlock. Bound and determined, she pounded with a hammer that she found, slamming harder each time, letting her anger and frustrations out while tears streamed down her face. The lock finally broke open. Amanda stared in stunned silence and disbelief. There, neatly displayed in front of her, was a collection of body parts and specimens, including Taylor's brain parts and eyeballs with root veins still attached, Brad's head with dark hollowed sockets, Jane and John Doe's heart, liver, uterus, and spine—all sterilized in glass jars, each revealing their gruesome tale.

Amanda screamed ceaselessly until her voice gave out. Minutes later, James ran down the hallway, entering the basement.

"What happened, Amanda? What is it?" he asked nervously, trying to catch his breath. "Why did you scream?"

Quickly becoming aware of her failed attempt to escape, James recaptured her in no time.

Moments later, a blood-curdling scream traveled from the basement through the hallways to the living room. James rushed frantically into the room, interrupting Camille's serene atmosphere.

"SHE'S GONE! SHE'S GONE!" he shouted. "Amanda is gone! I mean—she was gone!"

Camille was unruffled.

"Did you hear the birds chirping today, darling?" she said calmly. "I haven't heard them serenade lately," she pondered. "Hmm, what a pity." Then she returned to her reading.

"I—AM—NOT KIDDING!" James shouted. "When I went down to the basement, I found her cuffs broken, and SHE nearly escaped! Can you believe it?"

"What do you mean she IS—WAS gone?" Camille asked, flipping through the pages. "She either is or isn't." She glanced at James and continued. "Well, which one is it?" "WAS! I mean—WAS!" he clarified. "But I saved the day for you, my love!" he said proudly. Camille was now convinced James was explaining the situation accurately after all.

"Hmm... I might just pay her a visit," she muttered.

* * *

Moments later, Camille walked down the cavernous hallway that led to her basement. James followed behind. Hatred smoldered beneath her graceful surface; she masked her anger well. Perfectly calm and collected, the beautiful siren entered the room.

Amanda, again a prisoner, was terrified after seeing what Camille could do. As Camille moved near her, she wailed in a trembling voice. "I'm so sorry, Camille!" I didn't know what I was thinking!" she pleaded. "Please don't punish me! I beg of you! PLEASE!"

Touched by her emotional plea, Camille became magnanimous. Incredibly, she wrapped her arms around the troubled mother, cradled her, and offered her comforting words.

"Oh, come now, my darling. It's not your fault," she sympathized. "Everyone makes mistakes. We all do it—don't we, James?" She glanced at him. "There's absolutely nothing to worry about," she reassured her.

Camille's unpredictable behavior baffled James. Silently outraged, his face was a mixture of disbelief and disgust.

"What the devil are you doing?" he drilled at her. "Shouldn't you be mad at her?" he shook his head. "I don't believe this!"

But Camille believed in second chances. She felt a perverse moral obligation toward the grieving mother, a victim held against her will.

"You were once in trouble, too, James," she reminded, moving toward him. "Didn't you ask for my help then? She is just a lost woman." Then Camille quietly slipped behind the walls. Seconds later, she reappeared in the hallway. Like a beautiful leopard camouflaged against the walls of a dark cave, Camille, the nocturnal beast of prey—graceful yet powerful—leaped in a deadly pounce for Amanda's jugular.

Her fiery eyes burned with rage as she prowled toward her prey, armed with an antique iron crowbar. She had only one thing in mind: AMANDA. Savagely attacking her face, Camille struck repeatedly. Blood spattered on herself, the walls, and on the ground, leaving Amanda screaming in excruciating pain.

Seeking more than vengeance, Camille finally let out all of her demons gnawing inside of her ever since she was a child—only now realizing just how deep they were. She tore off Amanda's cheek, exposing her flesh and cheekbone, turning it from pale pink to bloody red in seconds—just like butchering livestock. Still, Camille hit Amanda's lifeless body, beating her to a pulp beyond recognition—even as her life force waned. Amanda was simply bludgeoned to her death.

For the coup de grâce, Camille took a stool and smashed it on Amanda's head with such force that it cracked her skull. Suddenly, a familiar voice interrupted.

"CAMILLE!" the voice shouted.

Camille, in a trance, halted for the first time.

"What?" she said absently.

Almost imperceptibly, she looked down at her dress only to discover something unsightly.

"Oh my God...my gown," she reacted impassively.

Her beautiful cream-silk gown was now stained with blood. And like a five-year-old, she looked up to James and added in a whispered voice. "She's ruined my gown. I best go up and change before dinner."

Camille rose up and walked away as if nothing unusual had taken place.

James was utterly speechless. Paralyzed, he retched up his lunch as he tried to sit down.

"God, help us all," he whispered, then passed out on the floor.

JAMES AND CAMILLE

Monte Carlo ~ London: 1999

17

It was not just the double life that Camille and James lived. The thrill of not getting caught was the most powerful drug in the dark market of their idyllic world. The constant anticipation, the adrenaline highs and the gratifying moments left them open to almost any precarious situation. Going above and beyond with charity donations gave them the alibi for their crimes. Their wonderful reputation kept investigators at bay, with no lingering suspicions linking them to their crimes—making Camille and James the most celebrated sociopathic couple in high society.

*   *   *

During an early Fall evening, Camille and James attended the exclusive Jewelry Auction Charity Ball for children. The black-tie event held yearly in Monaco attracted royalty, presidents, celebrities, and billionaires gathered by Prince Albert II—Invitation only.

For the Monegasque—the native language of Monaco still spoken by a small circle—gatherings of the rich and famous symbolized their rich heritage. During these events, locals took their families for long overdue holidays. For tourists, however, they were a powerful magnet. Thousands would camp out days ahead to witness events like the Monaco Grand Prix in the Spring. The Monaco Yacht Show had billionaires rolling out their yachts in the Fall. Monaco was an endless array of entertainment all year round.

* * *

A vintage Rolls Royce pulled up in front of the glamorous Casino de Monte-Carlo—an institution known for its decadence. Out stepped Camille and James, with crowds clamoring for their autographs from a distance. Striking alongside movie stars and royalty to the casino entrance, the two proudly walked the red carpet. Once again, all eyes were on the fashionable couple.

A charming British event director in his 40s greeted them at the front door. James and Camille were escorted to front-row seats. Donors brought soft hearts and cold hard cash to help save children in developing countries.

A short while later, the charity auction began as the world's rarest jewelry pieces appeared on a widescreen, and the bidding war began. Camille placed her bid on a one-of-a-kind Harry Winston sapphire and diamond necklace. Composed of step-cut emeralds framed with brilliant-cut diamonds, it had a detachable line of variously shaped sapphire and brilliant-cut diamonds at the front. Moments later, Camille was declared the winner of the coveted jewel.

* * *

Later that evening, donors and VIP guests gradually moved to the elaborately designed French ballroom next door for dinner. As they entered the lavish ballroom, an impeccably timed orchestra played inspiring classical medleys.

Statuesque silk draperies, gilded ceilings, and white lighting filled the room, along with long evening gowns and white tie and tails with trenchant mannerisms—reminiscent of the Golden Age of Hollywood. Moments later, a gracious host appeared on stage, reaching for the microphone.

"Welcome everyone to our 25th Annual Charity Ball Auction for children!" he announced proudly in a dignified voice. "We'd like to especially thank Le maître cuisinier Paul Bocuse for this evening's gastronomic delight on behalf of your Highness—Prince Albert II."

The crowd clapped loudly, nodding their respects to His Royal Highness Prince Albert II, then to the legendary Grand Master Chef Paul Bocuse. Then the band continued playing. A few meters away, surrounded by social acquaintances, Camille and James, were forced to socialize—a forte Camille had long considered her weakest, having been a recluse for a better part of her life. Coincidentally, her godfather, chef Paul Bocuse was circling the crowd when he came across Camille and James.

"Je pensais que c'était ma princesse, Camille!" said the master chef in French, asking if she was indeed his princess. In need of a rescue, Paul Bocuse's greetings could not have come at a more perfect time for Camille. The two immediately engaged in a warm-spirited conversation.

"Êtes-vous profiter de la nourriture ce soir?" he asked if she was enjoying his food. "Look at you, my dear...absolument magnifique!" he complimented, shaking his head with pleasure, then added. "If your mother could only see you now."

Camille was flattered. As if the god of food spoke the truth, she was humbled by his wise words. Like a doting grandfather, Paul Bocuse had long connected with Camille through their common love for gourmet meals. Always encouraging her to follow her dreams and to break the barriers, he told her to push those boundaries that awaited her in a limitless world, often comparing his cooking secrets and process to success. His words carried great honor for Camille. The two said their goodbyes, exchanging kisses. The grand master chef exited the scene.

Camille returned to her group when she was quietly interrupted again by the same event director, appearing from behind.

"Excusez-moi, Mlle Rogers," his voice whispered in her ear.

Camille listened intently as he spoke.

"I want you to say hello to his Highness once he's here; before you leave, of course," he added.

"Oui, oui...avec plaisir," she accepted graciously.

Minutes went by. The director returned with Prince Albert II himself beside him. Camille turned, and to her delight, she was met with alternating cheek kisses by the Prince. They chatted like old friends as if time had not passed them.

"Camille, how are you? It's been a while," said Prince Albert II in a courteous tone.

"Albert, darling—it's so good to see you!" an overjoyed Camille responded. "We're fine, thank you!" Then she presented James. "You remember Monsieur James Hughes, yes?"

"Yes, of course," the Prince acknowledged.

James reached for the Prince's hand.

"Hello again. It's very nice to see you," said James.

"Indeed. Good to see you too, James," Prince Albert II replied, then turned to Camille. "So, how's the diamond business?" he continued. "I hear you're working on a biopic about your mother."

"Just fabulous, darling," Camille remarked. "Life couldn't be better. And the biopic, well, there's more work to be done, but generally, it's going quite well. And the palace?"

"Same. Politics, life, the usual," the Prince replied. "You really ought to visit Camille, just like old times. You and James both. We'll have a nice dinner in the garden and enjoy the evening."

"That would be lovely," she smiled.

"Well, I should really go. Duty demands that I greet all the donors. You know how that is," Prince Albert II said.

"Yes, don't I know," remarked Camille.

"But I want to thank you, James, and your late mother once again for the tireless support you've given the children not only here in Monaco but all over the world." Prince Albert continued. "You really have a very big heart, Camille."

Camille was deeply humbled.

"Well, you know...anything for the kids," the heiress responded, winking back at him.

"See you later, darling," the Prince concluded. "Don't forget our dinner," he reminded, then walked away.

"I won't. À plus tard!" Camille reaffirmed.

Later that evening, Camille freshened up inside the powder room. Covered delicately in light pink-and-gold Cherub Toile wallpaper, the elegant restroom had lounge chairs at both corners infused with its fresh flower arrangement scents. A thoughtfully laid-out assortment tray on the wash counter was filled with: parfum, Eau de toilette, hairbrushes, perfumed soaps, fresh mints, and other amenities.

Camille touched up her red lipstick in front of a polished mirror. A frizzy-haired female attendant sat on duty in the corner, ready to hand out heated hand towels. The woman caught Camille's attention. Quietly dipping into her diamond-crusted evening bag, Camille pulled out a healthy wad of cash, all in hundred-euro bills, generously placing them on the cash tray on her way out. The attendant's eyes widened in disbelief. She wasted no time thanking the compassionate heiress for her gratuity.

"Merci pour le tuyau, Mlle!" She said in exuberance. "Vous êtes si bon! Bénisse votre cœur d'or! Bless you! God bless you, mademoiselle!" she continued to praise.

Bemused by the reaction, Camille turned around to explain herself.

"Oh, NO-NO-NO-NO!" she said emphatically. "Mon chérie, that money is to fix your hair!" she revealed. "Au revoir!"

Exiting the door, Camille left the attendant extremely perplexed.

* * *

At half past midnight back at the Chateau, Camille and James had a nightcap in their formal salon. Sipping Remy Martin Louis XIII Cognac, they relaxed in front of a majestic 19th-century Renaissance fireplace when James divulged his plan.

"You know, I've been in contact with people in London and other places about my work," he confessed. "They really want to see me."

Silently disappointed, Camille took a deep breath.

"And you've kept this all to yourself because—" she remarked. "I thought you wanted to be out, darling?"

"I know, but it's not as easy as you think," replied James. "I'm not like you, Camille. You're beautiful, strong, talented, and the daughter of a diamond legend who has more money than God." He continued. "Let's face it, you and I will never be equals." He then added soberly. "I'll always be the son of a servant. And deep down, you know I'm right. I've really thought this through, you know."

"But what's there to think?" Camille asked. "And how many more secrets are we keeping, James?"

"That's not fair," he replied. "It's not like that, Camille."

"How is it then?"

"You know," he hesitated. "I've been trying to get something going on my own since you've ruined my chances in Paris. The Art Gallery in Amsterdam called. This is a real opportunity, Camille," he stressed. I might even try the gallery in London, then go to the village to try to find my sister again," he continued.

"Amsterdam?" she asked surprisingly. "Have you lost your mind, darling? she continued. "They've got the worst prostitution in the red-light district, along with a thriving drug business like no other. There are bizarre things happening in Amsterdam, you know that!" she warned.

"And great artists like Van Gogh," James quipped.

"Who took a razor and sliced off his ear," retorted Camille. "Might I include his brother Theo and his sister, too?"

James shook his head.

"You're not going to stop me, Camille," he cautioned. I've already made up my mind, and I'm set to go!"

James stood and quickly swallowed his drink in front of the glowing fireplace.

"Well, have you met any of them?" Camille continued. "They're swinish buffoons—I can assure you that!"

James laughed.

"Yes, as a matter of fact, I have," he countered. "I've been to their bars, their restaurants, and yes, their peculiar nightclubs—if that makes you feel better. But you're right. People there can be weird. I'll give you that."

"Well, consider yourself warned, darling! That's all." Camille teased.

Seconds later, she quieted down, gazing steadily at the fireplace with the light reflecting back on her face.

CAMILLE

Monte Carlo: 1999

18

The following day, Camille's personal belongings were strewn helter-skelter all over her bedroom suite, including her diamond-studded evening pouch, designer shoes, expensive mink coat, and diamond watch.

James picked up after her one piece at a time. From the hallway to the lounge area, then the bathroom, the trail led him straight to Camille's master bedroom. Attributing her behavior to her recent travels, he thought nothing more of it.

James found Camille curled up in bed in a fetal position. She slept in her evening gown and looked despondent. Her reddened eyes, smeared with dried mascara, were swollen from crying all night long. Instantly, dropping everything, James rushed to her side. He climbed up on the bed, fully prepared to comfort her. Swathing his arms around her, he said, "hey, what's going on?"

Camille remained silent, reduced to tears as she stared back at him.

Yet James intuitively knew what this was about.

"Come on, my love," he comforted. "I'll only be gone for a few days. I swear, I'll be back as soon as I can, OK?" he added.

"It's nothing, James," Camille began. "I'm used to it."

"Used to what?"

"To people leaving me."

"Don't say that," he reasoned. "You know it's not true."

James realized how personal this was for Camille. A rare diamond—flawless and captivating from outside—Camille was in shards within. James could only give her a tighter hug. The heartfelt conversation turned from a serious talk to heavy drama.

"Oh, mon chérie, I would never leave you," James promised. "You're crazy to even think that."

"That's what my birth mother said when she gave me away," Camille replied tearfully. "That's what Jacques said...and what mother said," she hesitated. "That's what they all seem to say. Yet, everyone has left me."

"But that's in the past now," assured James. "And I'm here to take care of you now. Don't you see that? That's why I came back after so many years. I finally realize that I can't be without you, Camille. If you only knew how much I thought about you when we were apart," he hesitated. "So, they put us both through hell, and we both have painful childhood memories. And it probably scarred us for the rest of our lives. I get all that. But, we're still here, together." Then with conviction, he looked into her eyes and added, "I promise you no one will ever hurt us like that again. I won't allow it."

Camille shed further tears as dark memories unraveled from her past. "Why did papa do what he did?" she asked innocently. "Because of him, we had to bury a baby in the garden years ago. And mother, why was she so mean? When we were little James, I could never figure out why I've always liked the shape of a teardrop diamond. Even as a small child, I thought it was the most beautiful thing I had ever seen."

Fighting her tears, she continued. "Now I know it's just symbolically tragic, painfully interconnected with my life as if," she hesitated, "as if all this time, it was just a reflection of my own tears of sorrow. Moments like these, I wish I was never born." She took a deep breath and wept uncontrollably. "It just hurts, James. I'm so badly broken at times that some days I can't breathe!"

For the first time ever, Camille brought her heaviest and darkest burdens out in the open. She had been torn between protecting her mother's legacy and exposing the dark secrets in her family. Her mordant sense of humor hid a lost little child living in pain—longing to be loved like any other human. Bearing this cross her entire life, Camille was suffering deeply.

"I understand, my love. I really do," James responded.

The two quieted down for a moment.

"But then again, you won't be able to slice and dice, my love," he blurted out. "You can't pop eyeballs into glass jars, put your victims to sleep while wearing your gorgeous teardrop diamond necklaces and sipping on your fabulous martini cocktails—would you now?" he teased, "Gosh! What will I do without my Camille?"

Tickling her endlessly, the two went into peals of laughter like little children.

* * *

The next day, an unearthly wail echoed from the upstairs hallway. Camille cried out hysterically like a three-year-old, beseeching James to cancel his trip. Holding on to his ankle dearly like a ball and chain, she hung on every time he took a step forward, fearing total abandonment. Camille had officially lost her mind.

"You can't do this to me, James! I beg of you!" she vociferated. "Wait, wait!" she paused. "I'll give you my money, diamonds—anything you want! Just stay with me. PLEASE! James, you don't have to do this!"

"Camille, don't do this to yourself!" James warned. "This is so beneath you, my God! I really have got to go! I will call you as soon as I get there—all right?" Gently kissing her on the forehead, he looked into her eyes and said, "You take care of yourself now." Then he turned around and hurried out.

* * *

Two days later, James had returned from his trip and was discussing private matters with Camille in his office down in the basement. The two carefully studied the "before and after" photos of their fallen captives, neatly pinned up on a board next to the wall.

LILY AND JAMES

Monte Carlo: 1999

19

Days leading up to the annual Monaco Yacht Show, James was tidying up some throw pillows in the entertainment room when the doorbell rang. The home security monitor screen showed a young couple standing by the gate, waiting for a response.

"Bonsoir?" answered James from the speakerphone.

"Um, Bon-soir. I'm looking for…" the timid voice of a young lady said politely, in a slight British accent. "Mr. James Hughes?"

"Oui?" James responded, asking how he could help in French. "Comment puis-je t'aider?"

"He's supposed to live here," the young lady continued. "I've uh, I've come to visit him. I'm his sister."

A brief silence passed.

Lily Hughes, James' estranged sister, was a nineteen-year-old pretty blonde with a kind face. Good-natured and unassuming, she had neither seen nor spoken to her brother for many years. Standing next to her was her boyfriend, Chris. A handsome, well-dressed, gregarious young man in his early twenties, he had been eager to meet her family. Underneath his cocky façade was just a typical insecure man.

"Lily? Is that you?" asked James.

"James?" Lily replied, trying to remember his voice.

"OH MY GOD! It is you!" James exulted. "Well, how do you like that!"

"And guess what?" Lily interrupted. "I even brought my boyfriend with me for you to meet!"

"Well, come on in sis! I'll buzz you in, OK?"

"OK."

Seconds later, the automatic gate buzzed open. Lily and Chris entered the palatial property. Racing by the foyer, James threw the front door open and gave Lily a big hug.

"I don't believe it! My long-lost baby sister!" he swooned, shaking his head as he milled around her. "I sure have missed you so much!"

Lily was equally delighted. But her boyfriend Chris was feeling left out.

"Oh, I'm sorry!" James acknowledged, reaching out to Chris for a handshake. "I'm James."

"No worries, man. I'm Chris," he responded with an English accent, shaking back.

James then turned his attention back to Lily.

"Do you know how long it's been since I last saw you?" he continued. "I've been praying that someday you'll turn up! Now I know God sure works in mysterious ways!"

"He sure does!" Camille said aloud. Suddenly appearing, she slowly walked toward them, holding a martini cocktail as she ingratiated herself with the young couple.

"At least that's what my pastor says," she muttered. "Of course, he's full of shit if you ask me." Then returning to her normal voice, she smiled and said, "BUT—that's just me." Turning to Lily first, she introduced herself. "Bonjour! Enchanté! Je m'appelle Ca-mille...comment allez-vous?"

Immediately, Lily felt intimidated.

"Oh, I uh..." she hesitated. "We don't um...speak French," she added.

"I'm awfully sorry for you then, darling!" Camille teased.

Lily looked to Chris, confused. Both James and Camille chuckled.

"She's just pulling your leg," James explained.

"No, not yet, darling, that comes later." Camille winked at Lily. "James is right. I'm only teasing. Bienvenue au Domaine Rogers. You both are most welcome to our house!"

Lily let out a sigh of relief.

"Got it!" she said.

"Well, shall we move inside so we can all catch up?" Camille suggested. "It's getting a bit chilly out here."

"That would be nice," Chris replied.

Camille and James took the couple inside. Lily and Chris found themselves surrounded by wealth and luxury.

"And you, young man. I assume you're from England, too?" Camille asked Chris.

"Yes, ma'a—WHOA!" he halted. "You have got to be kidding me! So, this is how the rich and famous live?" he reacted, looking around the elegant lobby with low-hanging chandeliers.

"This is beautiful," Lily stared in amazement.

The four entered the opulent formal salon.

"It's very kind of you," Camille smiled. "Well, here we are. Of course, we can have drinks at the pool and watch the sunset," she proposed. "and have dinner here later."

"Splendid idea, my love!" James agreed. "Why don't we do that? We have heaters out there in case it gets cold."

"I don't mind," Lily said.

"How about I make us some martinis?" Camille offered.

"Oh, none for me, please," Lily replied. "I'm uh, I'm pregnant. Just water, I guess."

James lit up, glancing at Camille. "Did you hear that, Camille? I'm going to be an uncle!" he said.

"Congratulations, my dear," Camille acknowledged. "How far along, darling?" she asked.

"Oh, about three months," Lily smiled. "We actually just found out a couple of days ago."

"I tell you what," Camille said to Lily. "I'm going to make a special one just for you. Something in ruby red color with freshly squeezed juice without the booze, of course. How does that sound, darling?" She asked, winking at her.

"That sounds better. Thanks," said Lily.

"On second thought," Camille said to James. "I could use some help in the kitchen. I suddenly remembered I've sent the maids home early today."

"Why not," he said. "Anything to start this party—right guys?" he smiled both at Lily and Chris.

"I apologize, darling. It's just that I gave them one of those things— what do you call them again?" Camille asked of James.

"A day off, Camille. Geez," he replied with forced gaiety, glancing at the couple.

"Whatever, darling," she dismissed nonchalantly.

James rose up, and the two began to walk back inside the house. "Make yourselves at home, guys!" he yelled back.

"Surely, man. Thanks!" Chris responded.

* * *

Camille and James reached the gourmet kitchen. She put out elegant martini glasses and an expensive "Lalique" crystal punch bowl, resolute in celebrating the unexpected family reunion. James gathered ingredients, placing them on the marbled counter.

Throwing in liquid sugar, a dash of vermouth and fresh blood oranges, Camille stirred the bowl with a matching crystal spoon. Then she heated up cooked gourmet dishes placed in copperware, placing them on the stovetop and in the oven. Rummaging through several drawers, Camille was unable to find what she was looking for, then went back to cutting blood oranges. "Darling, where's that maple bottle I used the other day?" she said absently, with a tinge of frustration in her voice. "Oh, bullocks!"

"I don't know," James replied. "You're the queen of this domain. I surely wouldn't know where it is," he laughed.

Displeased, Camille headed over. "Don't be so cute, darling," she warned flatly.

"See those two out there?" she pointed her knife to the security home monitor screen. Each camera, bolted on four corner ceilings, showed the couple cuddling each other, enjoying the spectacular view.

"I don't trust any of them!" Camille continued. "Especially HER—your sister!"

"What? You're afraid she'll steel your cat or something?" mocked James.

"That's not it, Einstein!"

"Then what is it?"

James glanced back at the monitor screen.

"What's wrong with that picture?" he questioned. "Too happy? Too sad?"

"Don't you see?" Camille replied, unaware she was waving her knife dangerously close to him. "Just look at them. They don't have a care in the world. It's disgusting! In case you've failed to notice."

James' eyes followed the knife intently.

"You, um, you might want to watch that thing you're holding?" he cautioned.

But Camille completely missed the point.

"Oh, you mean—THESE!" She reacted, holding up one of the blood oranges and rolling her eyes. "Tell me about it! I've been telling those market people to stop giving me LO-SERS, but what're you going to do? C'est la vie!"

Hopeless! James thought. "Never you mind, Camille," he went to a specific drawer and opened it.

"Have you checked this one?" he said, spotting the bottle. "Well, now! What have we here? Looks like a maple bottle to me!"

Snatching it out of James' hand, Camille said. "Why don't you make yourself useful for a change. Get us some hors d'oeuvres—will you?"

"If you wish," James complied.

Suddenly Camille had a visceral feeling.

"I'm sorry, darling," she began, putting down her knife. "The last thing I want to do is to discourage you," she continued. "You know when something hits you in the gut and starts pounding heavily?

"What about?"

"Well, I have this nagging feeling that just won't go away," she revealed. "I would be totally remiss if I ignored it."

James sighed deeply, taking a moment to respond.

"Camille," he began in a sober fashion. "It's been a long time since my sister and I saw each other; you know the story," he reminded her. "Finally, she's back in my life, and we're together again—shouldn't I be celebrating that?"

Yes, darling. I don't disagree," countered Camille. "But an estranged sibling just showing up at your door unannounced—especially when she never bothered to answer your letters—don't you find her timing strange at all? Why now? Why not then?" she pressed suspiciously. "I just have a bad feeling, James. And it's not going away. I really hope you're right this time."

James had trusted Camille's instincts in the past, even when she turned out to be wrong. But he was not going to budge this time around. Sneaking up from behind, he embraced her lovingly, resting his chin on her shoulder.

"Come on, Camille, couldn't you at least be happy for me?" he persuaded gently. "Give me just this one? Please, my love?"

Slowly giving in, Camille smiled and turned around. "You know what darling? You're right! That's why I have you in my life—to keep me away from all the evil spirits in this God-forsaken world!"

Facing one another only inches apart. James then seized the moment by catching Camille off guard, gently kissing her on the lips.

"I love you, Camille," he blurted out, confessing his feelings.

Even more surprising, Camille kissed him back on the lips, though more like one might kiss a brother. "I love you too, James," she reacted coolly.

An awkward silence followed. James searched for her beautiful eyes, but she looked away. Then Camille broke out laughing and went back to stirring her punch.

"Fini, mon cherié!" she said playfully, announcing that she was finished. "All is dead and death for all," then winked at him.

James was thrown off balance.

"Well, come on then!" Camille beckoned, lifting her glass.

Moments later, the neighboring peninsulas were illuminated by distant city lights. Surrounded by a lush French garden, Chris and Lily sat waiting like lovebirds, enjoying the brisk wind. James entered with cocktails on a silver tray, trailed by Camille holding an elegant hors d'oeuvres platter.

"Don't fall in love just yet," she teased. "Have one of my fabulous martinis first. It's absolutely intoxicating!" she touted.

"Oh, Camille! You shouldn't have!" Lily said excitedly. "This is too much!"

"Oh yes, I should, and I certainly have," replied Camille. "You're our guests, remember? Better yet, a family member for a change," she continued. "I do have some fine "Beluga Caviar" just flown in this morning—if anyone cares to indulge?" she looked to both Lily and Chris. As neither had sophisticated palettes, the youngsters quickly declined the offer. Chris, the less adventurous of the two, was careful not to offend the hostess.

"Suona Esotico," he whispered to Lily in Italian, saying that it sounded exotic, but "God knows what's in it." Turning to Camille, he said, "Oh no, not for me, but I'll have one of those little thingies." He pointed to the platter of imported cheeses and cold meats.

"Ma il gusto è da morire," Camille replied back in Italian, saying the taste is to die for, surprising the couple. "Thingies?" she questioned.

"OH MY GOD!" Lily moaned. "You speak Italian, too?

"Among other languages, darling," Camille smiled.

"Chris is half English, half Italian!" Lily added proudly. "And he knows three languages! How amazing is that?"

"Camille speaks five," James interjected.

"What? That's unbelievable!" Lily said.

"Well, salut everyone!" Camille raised her glass. "I'll go fetch us some more hors d'oeuvres. Excuse me for a moment." Camille turned around and left.

"Cheers, guys!" James toasted to both Chris and Lily. "You picked a perfect night to visit. The weather hasn't been this gorgeous for a while," he said, then faced Lily. "And yes, Camille is one of the most talented people I know."

Seconds later, Chris pulled James aside to speak privately.

"Hey James, now that we're talking, do you guys, you um...party at all?" he asked.

"Party?" James asked quizzically. "Oh, you mean—I see," he smiled. "No, not exactly. Camille is not a fan. She doesn't like drugs or anything close, if you know what I mean." James explained. "She doesn't tolerate that sort of thing."

"Tolerate what?" Camille asked, now standing behind the two men.

"There you are!" James startled. "That was quick. I was just telling Chris that we don't party," he informed.

"Of course, we party!" Camille said aloud, turning to Chris. "I personally couldn't live without it." She passed the platter. "Hors d'oeuvres, anyone?"

James and Chris glanced at each other, bemused.

"No, Camille," clarified James. "What he meant was..." he began to gesture as if smoking marijuana. "You know..."

It finally registered on Camille.

"Oh, that!" she said. "Hmm, give these kids a break, James. It's only pot, for heaven's sake; what's the big deal?" she reasoned. "After all, this is the night to celebrate—right?" Then looking to Chris, she said excitedly. "Wait until you try his latest stash! It'll BLOW your mind!" Then pursing her lips, she blew a kiss, teasing in a thick Italian accent. "BELLISSIMO! MAMMA MIA! It's berry, berry good-ah!" Everyone laughed.

"Really?" Lily asked in a soft voice. "You really are the coolest, Camille—you know that? Now I know why James mentioned you so often in his letters."

"So, he did, huh?" Camille jested with a furrowed brow, glancing at him.

Everyone chuckled once again.

"Which reminds me, I will go and retrieve them right now," she said.

Minutes went by. Camille returned with marijuana, rolled in papers, and placed on a small elegant tray.

"Voilà!" she presented gracefully.

Heedlessly rash, Chris and Lily jumped in like two hungry wolves. They lit up the joints and smoked away. Camille and James stood watching from behind the glass garden door, amused by the couple.

"Shouldn't she be avoiding that?" Camille commented. "Considering she's pregnant?"

"It's too late now," James replied.

A few minutes later, they moved closer to the couple. Chris and Lily were now loose and relaxed.

"Camille, you really are the best!" giggled Lily.

"I'm glad you like it, darling," Camille said, then glanced at James. "So, shall we give our guests the pièce de résistance?"

"THE-WHAT?" Chris said aloud.

Lily burst out laughing.

"She means our dinner, back inside the house," James explained.

"Oh, that! I got you, man," Chris said playfully. "I thought for a minute there there she was talking about conspiring against the British. Bonjour, Monsieur...Mlle! You stupid British people! We won the war! GET OUT!" he jested, mimicking a French accent.

"No, my friend! Of course not!" chuckled James. "Quite the contrary. We're here to entertain you!"

The group laughed in unison. Carrying their drinks, they returned to the formal salon. All noticed the tantalizing aroma of Camille's dish permeating the house.

"It smells incredible, Camille," commented Lily. "Good thing I'm starved," she smiled. "I hope it's something good."

"Something good?" Camille reacted. "Oh, darling, you're looking at a connoisseur of the finest gastronomy worldwide!" she proudly stated. "Now, what can I tempt you with?" Hesitating for a moment, she then insisted, "Well, come on! TRY ME!" She winked at her.

Lily turned bashful.

"Actually, anything will do, Camille," she replied politely. "I just need to eat. Thank you, though."

"Speaking of which," Camille said, looking down at her watch. "Good heavens! I have to check on our dinner! Please excuse me again, everyone." Weaving her way to the kitchen, Camille suddenly stepped onto a large hammer hatchet left lying on the floor in the hallway. Enraged at the accident, she began to wreak havoc.

"DAMMIT, JAMES! UGH!" she exploded.

Within seconds, James raced down the hallway while Chris and Lily trailed close by. He saw Camille limping around with a swollen ankle trying to rise.

"Camille! Are you OK?" James asked alarmingly.

"Do I bloody hell look like I'm OK? MERDE ALORS!" she lashed out. "Why can't you put things back where they belong, huh? Now, look what you've done.

"You've twisted my ankle! Are you happy now?" she said to him angrily.
James felt diminished. "Really?" he began. "Cause, I can assure you I was entertaining just a moment ago," he retorted sarcastically.

"Don't you DARE be condescending with me!" Camille fumed.

"Wait a minute!" countered James. "You're the one who wanted to hang your artwork today—and so I did!" He then mimicked her. "Oh, James, darling, would you fix my chair, please? James, darling, would you fix my bed? James, darling, would you feed my cat Prince? And a million other things you make me run around for like a fool!" he added. "You know, I'm getting sick and tired of you blaming me for everything that goes wrong around here! And your attitude! You always boss me around like I'm your footman! Well, I've got news for you, DAHLIN'— mimicking her again—I AM NOT!" he said bitterly.

"YOU STUPID IDIOT!" Camille shouted, her eyes blazed with fury. "How many times do I have to tell you to mind your manners in front of strangers, huh? ARE YOU UNWELL?" Turning to Lily, she said calmly. "Lily darling, would you mind telling your brother that he should ONLY speak with me when spoken to? That's how we NOR-MAL people do it around here," she remarked cuttingly. "You see, he's been missing a few brain cells lately, which that has left him incapacitated. Officially making him, um, what's the term now—" Ruminating for a second, she turned to James and added. "Oh, I know! The RE-TARD of the day!"

"Normal? HA!" James retaliated with a wry expression. "You of all people! You're amazing; you know that? Stop acting as if you own me!

163

If truth be told, you never give me credit for anything that I do for you! It's like I don't even exist! But when you need something, it's Ja-aames!" he imitated her yet again.

"And YOU—are starting to sound like my pretentious father!" Camille shot back. "Better yet, my wretched mother! So, which one of the two are you, James? Cause either way—YOU DON'T IMPRESS ME!" she screamed in his face.

Chris and Lily felt terribly uncomfortable watching the two attack one another like mortal enemies. Ironically, James and Camille were the two most worldly people they had met, and at least until a minute ago, they surely knew more about protocols and etiquette than ten or twenty books written by experts.

"Um, hey guys," Lily interrupted subtly. "We're um; we're going to start heading back? We're not that hungry after all."

Then she quietly slid out of the room.

"Really, Camille, we're fine," Chris reiterated, following Lily out. "You guys have been swell. Seriously, we loved it. We've got to do this again some other time. Just call us, OK?"

"NONSENSE! STAY RIGHT WHERE YOU ARE!" Camille threatened like her mother, then stopped after she heard herself speak.

Chris and Lily froze.

"We're four civilized adults," Camille explained, composing herself. "And we'll have dinner as planned. Besides, there's an awful lot of food back there to eat alone," she jested. The others smiled, albeit weakly.

"James," Camille said to him.

"Yes, my love," he answered.

"Why don't you freshen up their drinks," she said. "See if they need anything while I put some cream on this ankle upstairs?"

"You got it," he smiled.

Life had returned back to normal in a flash. Camille limped her way to the elevator, then upstairs to her bedroom.

* * *

Twenty minutes later, Camille appeared at the end of the dining room hall while the others sat patiently in the living room.

"Everyone—dińer is finally served!" she announced.

"Excellent! I'm starved!" James rose up and said excitedly. "I'm going to wash my hands."

You need to use the lavatory as well?" he asked both.
Lily smiled.

"Nope. I'm good, man," Chris said.

And you, young lady," he beckoned to her. "Come with me."
Minutes passed. Lily returned from the bathroom without James.

"So, are we set yet?" she asked Chris, glancing back at the hallway. "Where's James?"

"I haven't seen him," Chris responded. "I thought you went together?"

"We did, but he told me to wait by the hallway and—"

"Hey guys," James called out.

His omnipresent voice came through the intercom speakers, reverberating around the house.

Chris and Lily were startled as they searched the room for James' elusive presence.

"James?" she asked curiously. "You sound weird. Like you're in a tunnel or something. Where are you, anyway?"

"Oh, I'm on the house intercom, sweetie," he replied. "Sorry, I disappeared on you guys. I had to run back quickly to the guesthouse and pick up some wine down in the cellar for Camille," he explained. "So, are you ready yet?"

"YEAH!" Chris and Lily answered excitedly, overlapping one another.

"Alright. So, turn to your left," James instructed. "See the black double doors straight ahead of where you're standing?"

Chris and Lily both glanced at the hallway, an endless stretch, given the size of the mansion.

"Where?" she asked.

"Which one?" Chris echoed.

Lily then spotted the door.

"You mean all the way down there?"

"I see it, too! There it is!" Chris pointed.

"That's right." James continued. "It's the French double Black Doors— the one with ornate gold trimmings at the far end. You guys see it?" he asked again.

"Yes?" both responded in unison.

"Well, walk toward it and enter only through that door." James directed further. "It's the formal dining room. Just keep going straight through the hallway until you reach the other side of the hall. You can't miss it," he continued. "I'll meet you in there, OK?"

"Uh—OK." Lily hesitated. "See you."

Chris and Lily began to walk the hallway. A profusion of luxury, the mini "Plaza de Glaces" of Versailles with a great art collection felt more like a scaled-down version of the Louvre Museum, but without having to buy tickets.

Enthralled by the surrounding opulence, they viewed paintings by Renoir, Van Gogh, da Vinci, Picasso, Rembrandt, and art sculptures by Michelangelo, Bernini, and Clodion until they reached the far end.

There stood eight-foot-tall black-lacquered double doors with ornate gold leaf trimmings; it was precisely how James described it. The two were hungry and excited.

"Well, shall we go for it?" Chris grinned.

"Yes, sir!" Lily complied, smiling.

"Well, here we go!"

Chris opened both doors. To their amazement, a rather familiar character wearing a black-and-white tuxedo and tie awaited them. James graciously waved them through the door as a doppelganger for the mystery man himself—Alfred Hitchcock.

"Good evening," he greeted in a typical Hitchcock manner.

"Good evening to you, my good sir." Chris smiled as he played along respectfully.

Lily was breathless. "Wow," she whispered, mesmerized as she looked around the room.

The most incredible vision, beyond their wildest imagination, laid before them: a perfect "winter wonderland" straight out of a best-selling fairy tale book. Suddenly, it was wintertime—cold and frigid. The room had been magically transformed into the early 1900s countryside of England, where legendary creatures like gnomes and translucent docile reindeer moved freely.

Subdued blue lights lit up one wall while delicate snowflakes dropped on a now densely covered salle à manger. The spellbinding imagery quickly seduced the willing couple. Infatuated by the fantastical illusion, Chris and Lily entered a dream-like state.

Seconds later, an old-fashioned gramophone began to play a muted "La Vie en Rose" by French singer Édith Piaf as though it was the 1930s all over again. The needle scratched against the record a few times before turning itself off, having run its course.

James watched closely as the couple moved toward the blue lights in complete wonderment, leaving their footprints in the snow. A new set of blue lights appeared on the opposite side, followed by a gleam of white burnish light subtly flashing downward. Then the beautiful heiress appeared aglow.

Goddess-like, she stood behind an elaborate dining table with gold candelabras on top while crystal chandeliers descended from the ceiling.

Dressed in her usual movie star attire with her red lipstick trademark, she served as the focal point of the room as though a Michelangelo sculpture.

With a beautiful mink fur shawl wrapped around her, she inhaled through a cigarette holder sharply evocative of Rita Hayworth in the movie poster "Gilda." The effects could not have been more dramatic.

But shockingly, decaying human parts used for adornments were placed on expensive china under silver dome covers—all beautifully paired up with luscious dishes like roasted Chicken and crowned Lamb.

The juxtaposition of Camille's glamorous appearance versus the grotesque platters horrified the already perplexed couple. Lily tried to react, but Camille spoke at the exact same moment.

"I've invited a few friends to join us," Camille began.

Equally revolting, a shocking number of well-preserved embalmed bodies sit peacefully next to each other as her guests. Affrighted, Lily let out a piercing shriek while Chris nearly threw up.

"AAAAAAHH!" she screamed.

"JE-SUS!" Chris followed.

"I take it that you don't like them," Camille commented dryly. She glanced at James as if to internalize for a moment. The two circled each other in peals of laughter.

"HAHAHAHAHAHA!" James guffawed. "That was great, Camille!"

"Darling, you know I couldn't resist!" she replied.

Naturally, Chris was appalled.

"You guys are so unbelievable!" he rebuked. "What's wrong with you two—huh?" Quickly turning his attention back to Lily, he saw her struggling to breathe.

"Are you OK, honey?" he asked in a concerned voice. Lily was hyperventilating as her face turned pale from the impact.

Gradually, the laughter died down.

"My God!" Chris exclaimed. "She's pregnant, for God's sake! Plus, she's got a heart condition!"

He then looked to both and said, "Why did you do it, huh? Are you guys sick? Look at her! She can't even breathe!"

"I don't think he appreciates our gesture James," Camille jested dryly.

Embarrassed by her comment, James cleared his throat.

"I'll get her a glass of water from the kitchen," he said in a sympathetic tone.

"Does this mean we skip the aperitif?" Camille interrupted innocently, glancing at both, waiting for an answer.

"Camille!" James admonished, then turned to Chris. "Do you think Lily requires medical attention?"

Lily struggled to whisper in Chris' ear.

No," Chris replied. "She doesn't want that. I only hope she and the baby are OK."

Shockingly, the tide turned. Dipping inside her purse, Lily pulled out a black PPK 8mm automatic pistol, pointing it straight at both Camille and James.

"That's it! I've had enough of you two lunatics!" she lashed out.

Camille's heart sunk. "Christ," she mumbled to herself.

"You're kidding me," said James.

"What astonishing behavior!" Camille remarked.

"And you have no one else to thank except yourselves—my heroes," Lily continued, giving out an artificial smile.

Still at a loss, James tried to catch up.

"What are you doing, sis?" he asked.

"Let me bring you up to speed, my brother," explained Lily. "We're here for one reason and one reason only—are you with me so far?"

"Yes, but Lily—" James reasoned.

"Shut up, big brother!" Lily cut in sharply. "You haven't told me what to do for ages, and you're not going to start now! This time I get to do the honor—and you know what you'll do for me?" she continued. "You're going to give up your part of your land even if it kills me. Got that?"

"What land?" James asked innocently.

"She means your share of the deed to this property, you fool," Camille quipped.

"You mean he still doesn't know?" Lily looked at Camille, then smiled in satisfaction.

Camille just shrugged it off.

"That's right!" Chris echoed. "Real estate business is by far and away the best investment these days. You two, of all people, know that." He then glanced at Lily, grinning. "We figured you both were worth the trip, buddy. And you know what? The woman is right! Ain't she a smart little cookie?"

Lily smiled at him charmingly.

"And with our baby on the way," she continued. "We can get married for sure; create a comfy family life here! And need I mention Camille's Private Jewelry Collection, which she inherited from her mother?" Lily divulged with a fiendish gleam in her eye. "Oh, YES! We know all about it!" she revealed proudly.

Lily made a hundred and eighty degrees turn from a sweet innocent sister to a cunning woman who could care less about anyone but herself.

"And, you guys think you can get away with this?" James commented flatly.

"What did I tell you earlier, James, huh?" remarked Camille. "I was right—was I not? Look at us, captured by a couple of neanderthals! Such behavior revolts me! Perdant!" she said with loathing in her voice.

Irascible, Lily headed over to Camille and pistol-whipped her on the face.

"Lady! You're testing the last of my patience here with that yakety-yak of yours!" she warned. At the same time, she began to feel lightheaded. "WHOA! Holy crap!"

Camille looked up, smiling as her lips bled. "What's wrong, darling?" she asked mockingly. "Feeling light lately?" Then mumbled under her breath, "You little putz."

Meanwhile, Chris started to lose his vision. With the dining area more distorted by the minute, he fell on his side. Oddly enough, he burst into a loud guffaw with giddy merriment, swirling his eyes up and around the ceiling like a four-year-old. He then dragged himself to a side corner and stared off into space.

"Just so you know, James, she wants Camille's jewelry collection" he slurred heavily. "Harry Winston...Chopard...Car, Car, Cartier in her mother's private collection room," he continued, almost unintelligibly. Facing Camille, he smiled. "Mu-must be good to be the jewelry heiress, huh?"

Chris had swiftly become a court jester; the man could not articulate a coherent thought to save his life. Camille and James glanced at one other, then burst into laughter.

"Darling, does this boy even know what he's babbling about?" Camille asked, turning to James. The two laughed even harder.

"SHUT UP! Both of you!" Lily replied angrily. "Enough of the wisecracks— all right? What did you do to him anyway, you freaks!" Turning to Chris, she demanded, "Get up, you fool! Here, tie up these two lunatics and place them in the closet," she tossed a bunch of zip ties over to him.

"Darling, aren't we being a little too dramatic?" Camille asked.

"Not quite enough!" Lily yelled. "And if you keep talking that way, they'll be more coming your way—how's that?"

"Um, guys, I'm still confused; what the devil we're talking about?" interrupted James. "Would someone care to explain what's going on, please?"

"I'll put it to you this way, my brother," answered Lily. "I know for a fact that you own half of the Estate—you follow me so far?"

"If you say so, OK." James hesitated.

"How do I know this?" Lily continued. "Because once upon a time, our beloved mother mentioned that Mrs. Rogers would be leaving half of this Chateau Estate in your name after she perished from this beautiful earth," she revealed. "That was under the condition that she first legalized you as her adopted son so her Princess Camille here would have someone to watch over her—I bet you didn't know about that, huh?" she paused with a wry smile. "You see, I've shied away from you, James, since you were always everyone's favorite." Then hardening her tone, she added. "It's the very reason why I ran away from the family many years ago. Now is that clear enough for you?"

"Exactement," agreed Camille. She then turned to Lily.

"And this, I suppose, is how you both repay our kindness? What did your mother teach you?" she added.

"Apparently nothing!" Lily cackled.

"I can see the charm," Camille quipped dryly. She then looked at James and said in a sober voice, "It's true, James. Our lawyer Mr. Brendon tried to locate and notify you and Mrs. Hughes for years after Mother died. But over the years, you kept moving to different addresses. London, Paris, Italy—he couldn't find you. The law firm finally gave up and turned the entire property over to me. I thought it best if I told you in the end," she reasoned.

"In the end?" James exclaimed. "Like in our dying hour, Camille? Is that the timing you had in mind?" he asserted. "God knows it sure isn't mine! Geez, I really need to sit down for this."

Lily's lightheadedness intensified. Lights and sounds swirled around her as she, too, began to lose control. Her hypersensitivity was painfully pronounced. Panic set in while Chris continued slipping back across the floor, mesmerized by visions on the ceiling.

"I know the demons and the dragons are comin' to take o'er!" he warned sluggishly. Then quickly shifting his finger to another corner, he pointed. "Look! They're ov'r there!"

Everyone turned. Chris was now pointing to a beautiful Renaissance painting of winged cherubs and flowers in a cloud setting on the ceiling. Facing

Camille and James, he asked innocently. "Do you have po-pool here?" Then added. "I'm so hot, I'm burnin', man!"

The two laughed at him even harder.

"Of course we do! Straight through that door, my friend!" James pointed.

Amazingly, Chris began to strip. He took his clothes off piece by piece, slowly dropping them on the floor while humming a seductive tune. Lily was so embarrassed that she finally had to look away.

"What're you doing, honey?" she asked, smiling faintly as she tried to cover him up.

"That's it!" Chris said sternly. "You can stay here if you wan' honey bunny, but I'm going in!" He darted across the room, flashing everyone with his glaringly naked pale butt.

"GOOD GOD!" Camille said with revulsion, looking away.

Plunging heavily into a gorgeously lit but freezing pool with a private terrace, Chris splashed the surrounding lounge chairs and pool umbrellas near the cabanas without a worry.

Muddled by her boyfriend's erratic behavior, Lily followed him out to the pool. Camille and James quietly observed from behind the sliding glass doors while Chris and Lily unraveled.

"Geez, I've never seen a guy so happy," commented James.

"Great, another dribbling idiot," Camille responded dryly. "I guess that's what 'Angel Dust' will do to you if you're not careful enough," she paused. "Maybe if we sit here long enough, they'll both start dropping dead," she added. The two laughed it off.

Minutes later, Lily walked back to the main house, grabbing a chair to sit down. "Somebody better get him out before that idiot realizes he can't swim!" she warned sternly. She then turned to James and said. "So, James, what're we going to do about it, huh?"

"About what?" he replied.

"About your land? YOUR share, remember?" Lily said. "Or must I spell everything out for you?"

James let out a sigh. "But that doesn't even make any sense, Lily, and I'll tell you why," he explained. "Assuming half of it is mine, right?"

"Yeah, I'm listening," Lily nodded suspiciously.

"Camille still owns the other half—don't you see?" continued James. "Christ! She only owns a multi-billion-euro diamond jewelry company and almost half of the Real Estate in Monte Carlo. Hell, she practically owns the very air you and I breathe. The woman has more money than God! How're you going to manage that?"

"It's all right, James," Camille said resignedly. "I'll sign over my half of the property as a gift to her."

"Camille—DON'T." James shook his head. "What if they don't stop here?" he said. "Worst yet, they'll kill us, anyway? What leverage do we have then?"

Camille discouraged him with a look. Respectfully, James backed down.

"Um, it really pains me to break up this sweet talk of yours, but don't you get it by now, James?" interrupted his avaricious sister. "We're a family!" she continued, giving out a mirthless laugh. "Man, I still got to teach you such things? Why would I want to kill you?"

Then a volley of sharp noise hit Lily again. "DAMN IT!" she shouted. "Could someone stop that BLOODY noise?"

"What noise?" James responded.

"We best give her the property," Camille said. "They won't go away until they get what they want."

"That's right bitch! THANK YOU!" Lily remarked sharply. "Finally, someone gets it around here! No wonder she has all the jewels!" she said to James.

"You better fish out Bozo," Camille instructed James, "so they can be on their way." Turning to Lily, she said, "It'll take me a few minutes to search for the documents you need. They're in my upstairs office. My attorneys usually handle all of my business affairs, including the Trust and Will, the company's financials, and my real estate holdings—as you can imagine," she explained. "We certainly don't want to confuse this transaction with my Monte Carlo real estate residences and luxury homes."

"You mean the line of condos on the hillside?" a wide-eyed Lily asked. "You own those too?"

"And the Compagnie Monégasque de Banque, the Banque J. Safra, the BNP Paribas Private Bank, the Credit Suisse and the UBS in downtown Monte Carlo, who all rent out her properties," James added.

"Geez! Just when I thought I hit the jackpot. Whoo-hoo!" she exhilarated. "You guys are the gift that keeps on giving! I can't wait to tell Chris about this!" she said, then looked at Camille. "So, do your thing, honey, 'cause I got all the time in the whole world!" she grinned.

"As you wish," Camille said.

But James remained unconvinced. "I don't know," he shook his head. "I really think this is a bad idea."

"I THINK NOT!" Lily shouted back. Then her body began to writhe, jerking backward and forward, a little too painful for James to watch.

"OHHH—MY—GOD, help me!" Lily cried out, her body shuddering all over.

James stared in sheer astonishment. "Um... Camille," he said, his attention rapt solely to Lily. "I think you better take a look at this!"

Seconds passed. The two roared in laughter, barely containing themselves. Lily was twisting and turning uncontrollably. Finally submitting to her struggles, Lily died a painful, mysterious death.

A startling buzz came through the intercom wall speaker. Camille was visibly alarmed.

"What was that, James?" she asked nervously.

"Someone is at the gate," James replied.

"I know that, you fool!" she retorted sharply.

"But we better find out who it is first; go on from there."

"Fine, you go first."

James moved toward the intercom speaker and pressed the button.

CARLTON

Monte Carlo: 1999

20

In the growing darkness, the city of Monte Carlo glistened by the harbor. Carlton, wearing a buttoned-down dress shirt with a windbreaker jacket, found his way to Camille's Chateau. Determined to get to the bottom of what he uncovered days prior, he thought the best way to remedy the situation was to do good old-fashioned police work. And so good old-fashioned police work Carlton did.

After instructing his daughter Jesse to stay at the hotel, Carlton felt emboldened and was in his full investigative work mode. An hour later, he stood in front of an enormous black gate, speaking with James on the security phone.

"Bonsoir?" James answered calmly.

"Um, Bon-bonsoir," Carlton began in an amateur french. "This is Special Agent Joe Carlton from the United States Federal Bureau of Investigation? I was wondering if Camille Rogers and James Hughes might be available to answer a few questions?" he continued. "It will only take a few minutes."

James released the button. "It's the FBI," he said to Camille.

"The FBI? What're they doing here?" she fretted.

"I haven't a clue."

"Well, should I call my lawyer?"

"It's probably nothing," dismissed James. "We should see what he wants. You know how these guys can get."

"No! I don't!" she whispered sharply. "It's not like we have them for tea every day!"

"Fine, so it's our first time," he rolled his eyes.

A brief moment went by.

"I have it!" Camille perked up. "Why don't you ask him what this is about?"

"OK, that's good!" James agreed. He then pressed back the button. "What is this in regard to, may I ask?"

"Ah yes, it's about missing mother and daughter tourists last seen around your neighborhood this past summer," the agent replied. "Long and short of it, the Monaco Police referred me to James and Camille as leading locals who might be able to assist."

James let go of the button. Camille's heart raced.

"Sounds like it's just routine questioning," James said. "If we don't deal with it now, it might raise suspicions." He then added. "Should I let him in?"

"Wait a second!" objected Camille. "Let's think this through for a minute, shall we?"

Both pondered for a moment, each studying the other's face as they thought over the best way to handle the situation.

"I don't know, darling. I really think we should call my attorney," she suggested once again. "After all, this is a double homicide case—don't you think?"

James could not disagree more.

"I'm telling you, it's only going to create a cloud of suspicion if we don't do it now," he implored.

"Um, hello?" Carlton's voice interrupted from the intercom.

Feeling pressure to respond, James pressed Camille for an answer with a look. Given so little time to decide, she shrugged her shoulders. Taking matters into his own hands, James returned to the intercom and spoke freely.

"Yes, agent Carlton," he responded. "I apologize, but I um... I'm not at the main house right now," he continued. "I have to walk down to the guesthouse to let you in. Can you give me a few minutes?"

"Yeah-yeah, no problem. I'll wait," Carton replied.

James released the intercom button for the last time.

"BLOO-DY FBI!" Camille let out furiously, then composed herself. "You better hide Bozo and his girlfriend first before those clowns get us in trouble," she instructed firmly. "Meantime, I'll go freshen myself upstairs—all right?" She turned around and hurried her way upstairs.

"We're already in trouble," James muttered to himself.

* * *

Two days prior to his visit to the Chateau, Carlton and his daughter Jesse made it to town. Around late September, the Monégasque welcomed thousands of tourists for the Monaco Yacht Show celebration at Port Hercules. Tourists flocked en masse, trying to find a spot to settle in. For four straight days, restaurants, nightclubs, casinos, and shops would hit the roof in sales. Elite visitors attending a plethora of glamorous events and VIP parties were guaranteed to have a fine time. Memorable experiences were compiled like a book in every visitor's heart, waiting to be passed on for generations to come.

Monégasque and their offspring sailed small boats near the dock on that bright sunny morning. A string of adorable children trailed along in canary mini-boats while parents and guardians observed nearby. A vast collection of expensive yachts sailed out of the Monaco Harbor, making it the largest water exhibit on the European continent. Spectators drank in the scene as one phenomenal cruiser after another floated by.

Off in the distance, a young female redhead observed the festival through her binoculars. A yacht painted with a unique diamond-studded tuxedo design suddenly engulfed her view. Quickly sharpening her lens, she took in its enormity and name: DIAMONDS ARE FOR COCKTAILS.

Camille and James appeared in view, lounging on their tri-level deck in chic pool attire, sipping cocktails. Servants catered religiously to their needs. Private pools, a helicopter pad, jacuzzi, bar, and outdoor movie screen screamed luxury.

Heading out for a quick tour in St. Tropez, Camille and James were on their way to a huge gala held inside a private castle vineyard owned by one of Prince Albert's friends. They were not only living a glamorous life but were the envy of all.

James, leaning back on a lounge chair, placed his hands behind his head, interlocking his fingers. Lifting his feet up, he crossed both his legs.

"Ah," he sighed, smiling. "This is what life is all about."

A moment of silence. Basking under the glorious sun, the two relaxed as they sailed toward the French Riviera horizon.

Fascinated, Jesse followed the yacht through her binoculars. Watching scenes unfurl, she sat opposite her father, Agent Carlton, brunching at a café bistro terrace facing the thrilling harbor.

Carlton, sipping his aromatic espresso, was reading a local entertainment paper when he discovered something that could potentially blow his case wide open.

"Well, I'll be DAMNED," he muttered, greatly surprised.

"What, daddy?" exclaimed his daughter. "What happened!"

"Uh, sorry, sweetie," Carlton replied. "It's nothing. Daddy might've found what he was looking for, I think."

"Like a present for mom?"

Carlton smiled. "Even better, sweetie." he said. Then turning quietly to the harbor, staring blankly out to sea, he dropped his voice down to a whisper. "Even better," he repeated.

* * *

Back at the majestic gate, Carlton heard a loud buzz, then walked inside the palatial property. Wonderstruck by the wealth, he eventually reached a red lacquered door and pressed the doorbell.

"Hi there," James swiftly greeted. "You must be Special Agent—"

"Joe Carlton of the FBI," Carlton finished.

"Please, come in!" James reached for a handshake. "I'm James. James Hughes," he introduced himself. "I live at the guesthouse at the end of this property. Sorry, you caught me in the middle of something."

Carlton seemed lost.

"We had guests earlier," clarified James. "But everyone has left. And I was tidying the place up."

"I see," Carlton replied, looking around the property. "I apologize for showing up unannounced," he reasoned. "I hope I didn't come at a bad time."

"Everything is a bad time when you're busy, Agent Carlton," James countered.

"Touché," Carlton smiled. "Honestly, I didn't even plan on doing this today."

"Neither did we," Camille said aloud.

Charming and cordial as ever, Camille was back in form as a marvelously cool heiress, beaming with confidence. A far different woman than just moments ago.

"But no worries," she continued. "We're accustomed to surprises around here." Flashing a smile at Carlton, she turned to James while placing a cigarette in her mouth. "Isn't that right, darling?" she said.

Carlton was completely taken by her.

"Indeed, we are," James smiled faintly, rushing to light her cigarette.

"Thank you, darling," Camille puffed away. Then looking the agent straight in the eyes, she introduced herself. "Bonjour. Je suis heureux de vous avoir rencontré. I'm Camille Rogers," she said, pleased to have met him.

"Bon-jour. Nice to meet you, ma'am," Carlton replied. "I'm Special Agent Joe Carlton of the FB—" he halted. "Wait! You're Camille? The one I came here to see?" repeated the agent.

"Yep, she's beautiful—isn't she?" remarked James.

"Who did you expect, Agent Carlton? A sharp-toothed fairy, all the way from the F—B—I?"

An awkward silence followed. Carlton looked away in search of a response.

"Um..." he cleared his throat. "I really didn't know what I was thinking," he admitted bravely.

James then chuckled. "No worries, Camille likes to play around."

"I can see that," Carlton cracked a smile.

All three finally broke the ice.

"So, to what do we owe the pleasure, Agent Carlton?" asked the heiress.

"Uh, yes, ma'am," he responded. "I just need to square away a few details from this case I've been working; if you two don't mind?"

Camille tried to read the agent's mind for a moment, then continued. "It must be important then."

"Yes, ma'am. It is."

"D'accord," Camille proceeded. "Very well, why don't we all go inside so Agent Carlton will be more comfortable."

"I agree," James said.

Camille ushered the group into the hallway.

"Thank you, Mrs. Rogers. I appreciate it," Carlton mentioned. "This won't take very long, I promise."

"Miss Rogers," she corrected. "You said MRS."

"I apologize, ma'am," he responded.

Tucked in a dark corner, a fascinating set of eyes panned the scene gleaming like diamonds—as though the latest ad campaign for L'Allure. Camille's feline, decorated with a sparkling diamond collar, quietly observed.

"Phew! Nice house!" Carlton exhaled.

"That's very kind of you, Agent Carlton. Thank you." Camille accepted graciously. "It belonged to my family. Diamonds, real estate," she explained further.

"But who's counting, right?" James smiled.

"I guess no one!" chuckled the agent. "Wait a second!" he exclaimed. "You are the adopted daughter of the late Claire Rogers?"

"In flesh and blood, my friend!" replied James.

Camille's cat began to circle around the agent's leg as if wanting attention. Carlton stopped walking. Camille went down on her knees, and the cat immediately climbed up, settling in her lap.

"What are you up to, my darlings?" she petted gently. "Good boy, very good boys." She then looked up to Carlton and said. "My cat really likes you, Agent Carlton. I hate to admit it, but believe me when I say this is RARE."

Though slightly confused, Carlton decided to pet the cat just to please Camille.

"Hi, guy—how's it going?" he asked, feeling the softness of its fur. "Boy, aren't you beautiful," he added.

The cat gave back its overly satisfying purrs and then turned to him, revealing its face. To his horror, Carlton saw a sinister-looking feline born with two faces melded together like a Siamese twin, two mouths, two noses, one eye brown and the other blue. Carlton sprung back like a jittery fool.

"JEE-SUS, SWEET MOTHER-OF-GOD!" he said nervously. "What in God's cruel earth is that?"

With a humorless look, Camille glanced at James. Carlton quickly realized that neither one was laughing.

"Something wrong, Agent Carlton?" asked Camille in a deadpan voice.

"I-I'm sorry," Carlton stammered. Realizing that he had made a fool of himself, he tried to calm down. "I uh, I didn't mean to um—" Then trailed off. "Cute cat! What's his name—I mean their names, of course?" he quickly corrected himself, smiling faintly.

"That's all right, Agent Carlton," Camille said, scooping up her feline. "He never fails to get attention. "One side is Monte, and the other is Carlo," she revealed. "I found him behind the dumpster outside of the Jimmy Z Club. And guess in what town?"

"Monte Carlo?" Carlton hesitated.

"Bingo!" she exclaimed. "He was badly beaten with broken paws, burned skin, cuts all over. I decided to take him home."

"That's very noble of you, Miss Rogers," Carlton said. "Few heiresses care about anyone but themselves."

"Thank you, Agent Carlton," she acknowledged. "I wanted to make a difference."

"And it sure did," added James. "Since they're definitely God's gift."

"We all are darling, we all are," Camille replied. She then put her cat down. "Well, here we are."

All three finally reached the living room.

"Shall we all go into the family library?" James suggested. "It might be quieter."

"Marvelous darling!" Camille agreed.

"This will be fine," Carlton said. "You have been kind to invite me in. I'll make it quick."

"Why don't we get a drink first?" Camille suggested, swinging around the elegant marble bar counter.

"Would you like a cocktail, Agent Carlton?" she offered.

"Camille, can't you see the guy is working?" James said. Turning to Carlton, he continued. "Sorry, Agent Carlton, Camille gets excited when entertaining guests. She's a terrific hostess, if truth be told."

"Is that right?" Carlton remarked, then graciously declined Camille. "No, I'm good."

"Nonsense!" Camille insisted. "I make a MEAN martini! Tell him, James!" She looked to the agent yet again. "You are in the French Riviera—are you not?" she asked.

"I believe so, ma'am," Carlton replied timorously.

"Well then—you deserve one!" she said aloud. "Come on, live a little, Agent Carlton! I usually don't insist, but I've been told they're to die for." She winked at him and proceeded to mix a few drinks.

"We're not rigid here like you Americans, Agent Carlton," she said bluntly. "You tend to get bogged down on trifling matters. Things that need not concern you—frivolous things," she said, continuing her work. We on the French Riviera, by contrast, like to keep things loose around here; flexible as they say." Looking up with a big smile, she added. "We simply celebrate life! Voila!" Her French martini cocktails were suddenly ready.

"So how about it, Agent Carlton?" she pressed again.

"Really, Agent Carlton, you must try it," James insisted. "Camille's signature cocktail includes a billionaire's vodka she had especially distilled from France, the freshest pineapple puree and blood orange juice, and a dash of Chambord liqueur with a twist of lemon. Now, how bad could that be?"

"Put it this way, once you've tried and liked it—you might never experience it again." Camille persuaded further. "Come on!"

Carlton, who managed to hide his alcohol abuse from just about everyone in his life, was a functioning alcoholic. But pressed by Camille, his sharp detective instincts failed him. Once a highly-regarded agent and doting father, he now carried defeat on his shoulders. His best-kept secret: A drink can always help.

From embarrassing blackouts and memory lapses to violent behaviors that threatened his work and marriage—and even disappointed his biggest fan—his daughter Jesse, Carlton was a different person once inebriated.

Literally serving as the standard-bearer for the Academy, Carlton was a role model for agents in training. His prior track record won him countless awards, recognitions, and honors that broke records all across the board.

With that in mind, the Bureau never lost sight of his ability to solve the toughest crimes during his forty-year tenure in the intelligence community. Many Alcoholics Anonymous meetings later, Carlton was able to keep his job.

But when Carlton learned the devastating news about his daughter's life-threatening illness—his darkest days lay ahead of him. He was yet to discover how deeply he had fallen into the black hole that eventually overtook his world.

Time and again, he endured insuperable pain thinking about his daughter, believing he was cursed by God. The convenient forgetfulness engendered by alcohol was his only solace. Yet Carlton realized he could either sober up and witness his daughter's inevitable death with honor or take the coward's way out by drinking himself to death.

For the past two weeks, after his boss forced him to spend time with his daughter, Carlton surprisingly lived up to his promise to himself—avoiding alcohol and cigarettes all the way to Monte Carlo.

Now in enticing company with alluring surroundings, Carlton once again found himself conflicted by alcohol.

"That good, huh?" he vacillated, slowly rocking back and forth.

"Oh yes, Agent Carlton," James replied. "Trust me when I say it's good."

"Or WE wouldn't be offering it," Camille quickly echoed.

"That makes sense." He first looked to James, then to Camille.

Carlton knew taking a swig would be a cardinal sin. Still, all he could think about at the moment was that French Martini cocktail. He didn't care if it contained gasoline.

"Oh, what the hell!" he relented. "You both got me! Besides, I'll just have a sip or two—it can't hurt, right?" he tried to convince himself. "I just want to experience that delicious juice taste. After all, I'm here on vacation at the French Riviera and NOT on duty!" he revealed.

"Oh? How's that?" Camille asked in a curious tone, handing Carlton her luscious cocktail, then giving one to James. Taking the third glass, she sat beside the agent.

Carlton sighed. "Nah, I don't want to bore you guys. It's a long story."

"No, please tell us, Agent Carlton," Camille encouraged. "We really want to know."

"OK," Carlton began. "So, I've been stressed lately that my boss gave me time off to take care of my daughter. More to the point—why I drink," he admitted in a shameful tone. "I'd been digging back into the case of two American tourists gone missing this past summer and working with local Monaco authorities, so I decided to bring her to Monaco."

"You're daughter?" Camille replied curiously. "What about her?"

"She's um...." Carlton hesitated, fighting back his tears. "She's uh... been really sick. Only fourteen years old and terminally ill with Acute Myelogenous Leukemia. It affects her bone marrow and blood but went undetected for at least a year," he continued. "The doctor said that if she's lucky, she'll make it to a third year. Bringing her here fulfilled one of her lifelong dreams. She always wanted to see the boats in Monaco." Then he broke down. "It's the least a father could do," he sobbed.

"That's horrible, Agent Carlton!" Camille sympathized. "I'm awfully sorry for your loss!" She picked up his glass and handed it to him, raising hers. "Cheers! For what it's worth, it will help you smooth out the edges."

"She's not dead yet, Camille!" James said sharply. "Cut the guy some slack." He then turned to Carlton and continued, "And yes, that's terrible news, Agent Carlton. We're truly sorry to hear of your misfortunes."

James, too, raised his glass. "Here's to more blessings to your family coming your way!"

"Like the wife gets it next?" Camille quipped dryly. "That would be a SUPER blessing then."

James and Camille remained silent as they quietly sipped their cocktails.

"I uh, I'm really touched by your sentiments, guys," Carlton smiled. "And to think, I just met you two." Then putting on a serious face, he pulled out a small pad from his side pocket, quickly scanning his notes. "Anyway—where were we?" he resumed.

"Back to business, I suppose?" Camille replied, glancing stealthily at James. "So, how can we help you, Agent Carlton?" she asked.

"Well, just to backtrack a little," as I said, the Bureau was actively investigating the case of two missing Americans here in Monaco. A mother and daughter named Amanda Collins and her fourteen-year-old daughter Taylor, both from Los Angeles. They went missing only days after their arrival." He then looked up to both and asked. "You may have heard about it in the news?"

Each shook their heads gradually.

"No, not really," James answered, then looked away.

"Never heard of them," blurted Camille. "But then again, we're not big on news around here, Agent Carlton. It's a very quaint town."

"And um, Monaco police would have the jurisdiction to investigate beyond, even places like France had a crime been committed there," James added nervously. "They would've paid us a visit by now—I would think?"

Barely holding it together, James seemed more upset by what the agent did not know versus what he did know. He felt the blood slowly drain out of his body, and his bowels were cold with fear.

"I know that, Mr. Hughes," Carlton responded in a serious tone, unbuttoning the top part of his shirt as he noticed their reactions. "It's actually a combined effort between our Bureau, the local authorities,

Interpol, and intelligence agencies all over the world. That's why I'm here," he paused. "Let me ask you this—you two do travel a lot? Yes?" he asked.

"Yes," James replied dubiously.

"How often are you here in Monte Carlo?" Carlton added.

"Often, of course!" Camille answered. "Who wouldn't, for heaven's sake? It's the best place on earth!" she boasted. "Any mad dog or moron would see that."

"But, what has this case got to do with us, Agent Carlton?" clarified James.

Carlton hesitated, then continued. "An exotic car you both drive has been linked to the case I'm investigating," he disclosed. "More specifically, to the registered owner of this vehicle named, wait, I have it right here." Flipping through his notepad, he continued, "The Bright Lights Productions Company which you both own. Um, can anyone explain that?" he said nonchalantly, downing the last drop of his martini. "PHEW! This is really good stuff, Camille!" he exclaimed. "You were right about this one! Boy, it's DELICIOUS!"

But Camille's resolve was unshakable. Analyzing the agent in return, she stood coolly and remained ten steps ahead of the game. She knew exactly how to outmaneuver the witty agent. Camille was the perfect chess player.

"And this is why you came, I gather?" she replied with confidence.

"I guess! What else is there, right?" Carlton laughed annoyingly, then looked to James. "Boy, it's hot around here! Is the air on by any chance?" he asked. "I don't know why but—I'm HOT!" He looked at Camille next and added, "Wow, I can't believe how good your martini wa—" Giving out an embarrassingly loud belch, Carlton laughed. "Whoops! I'm so, so sorry! Or should I say—excuse moi, mademoiselle?" Then he chortled like a fool.

Deeply repulsed by his uncouth behavior, Camille was tempted to retaliate but instead gave James a furtive glance.

"I um, I guess I better go check the temperature," James said. He rose up and exited the room.

Camille immediately followed. "I need to use the ladies room," she announced, leaving the agent all by himself.

* * *

A short time later, the inebriated agent walked into the formal salon. Wandering aimlessly, he spotted what looked like a spec of dried blood on the marble floor, which aroused his concern. Turning off the nearest light, he immediately began his investigative work. Applying it evenly in the darkness, he sprayed a reactive chemical substance called "luminol," trying to positively confirm the blood.

Seconds later, traces of human blood corroborated his suspicion. Matching at least Taylor's or Amanda's DNA sample back at the laboratory was all he needed, and he had enough evidence to close the high-profile case. Carlton turned the lights back on, then sunk back on the opulent sofa and dozed off. He hadn't the faintest idea how long he slept or if the two had forgotten about him. It all seemed to blend in.

Several minutes passed. Camille returned and saw the agent slouching with interlocked fingers on top of his stomach, his eyes closed. She rejoined him on the sofa.

"Are you all right, Agent Carlton?" she asked.

At first, Carlton heard an angelic voice echoing from a distance. Then turning to her, he grinned lazily as thoughts percolated through his mind.

"Huh?" he mumbled to himself, fluttering his eyes open. Instantly, he dusted himself off, shaking his head. Carlton suddenly realized he had fallen asleep while they were gone.

"I was saying that I do have other engagements I must attend to tonight," Camille repeated. "So, if we're done here, Agent Carlton, I'd rather you—"

But Carlton could only grin back stupidly.

"Don't you worry about it, honey," he dismissed nonchalantly as if a different person. "I do have one more question, though."

"What is it, Agent Carlton?" Camille asked.

Scooting next to her, he looked her straight in the eyes and added freshly. "So, Camille, sweetheart."

"Yes, Agent Carlton?"

"Oooh! It's so formal around here!" he teased. "I like that!" Then continued.

"Just call me Mick, OK? I think it's better—don't you?"

Camille was genuinely confused. "You mean, Joe?" she clarified.

"Who's Joe?"

"Never mind."

Camille knew she was in imminent peril with the ever-changing agent. Something was percolating in the air, yet she had the wits to play along.

"You have a question, Agent Carlton?" she reminded him.

"Oh yeah, that's right," he perked up again. "So, how in the world did you acquire all these riches?" he pried. "I mean, just look around you—MAN! You're like Queen Marie Antoinette in your own Versailles Palace!" Grinning back to her, he slowly nodded. "You've got to admit, that's an awful lot of money—HONEY!" he taunted.

A deeply surprised Camille flinched back. Grappling with the agent's directness, she felt powerless for the first time.

"How do you mean, Agent Carlton?" she replied.

"It's really a simple question, you see," repeated Carlton, cozying up to her. "Again, what'd you do to acquire this palace—SWEETHEART? Who did you have to sleep with around here? Did you do some kinky stuff to him?" he tried one last time. "Oh, come on! You can tell me! WHO DID YOU HAVE TO SLEEP WITH, HUH?" he shouted at her.

Camille was beyond horrified. She remained paralyzed. Just when she thought Carlton was despicable, he took his perversion to a mind-numbing level of anathema. Throughout her life, she had loathed people like him.

But for a law enforcement detective whose primary duty was to protect and serve, it was a travesty. Pushing further, Carlton brazenly placed his hand on top of her one leg like Jacques used to do.

"I bet you did—you little dickens, you!" Carlton grinned. "You little whore!"

Camille shuddered at the thought of letting another sexual predator violate her, if only with words. Yet to her surprise, she folded like a five-year-old. Her eyes swelled as her heart raced faster than she could breathe. She sat there motionless, frozen in terror. A torrent of emotions he had forced open her floodgates.

"Stop it! Stop it! DON'T TOUCH ME! GET AWAY FROM MMEEEEEE!" she screamed, coiling up on the other end of the sofa, curling both knees beneath her.

James raced downstairs in a series of flying leaps. Deducing what happened based on Camille's look of terror, his face was unmistakably unforgiving.

"What're you doing, Agent Carlton?" James stuttered in disbelief, suppressing his anger. "I thought you were here to investigate? Help find those missing children so they might return safely to their homes. Give them the proper love and care they deserve, especially those suffering from child abuse," he paused. "I turn around, and you assault my Camille?" Moving closer to him, he then raised his voice. "Who do you think you are? We've let you into our home, treated you as our guest, and answered all your questions. What more do you want?" he shook his head. "This ain't right!"
Astonishingly, Carlton offered no apology.

"Don't be alarmed, man—" he dismissed casually. "We uh, we're just playing here," he continued. "You know how it is, just a silly game! Really!" he cracked a smile.

But James stood utterly unconvinced.

"Sure, Agent Carlton," he replied impassively. "I believe you like I believe our neighbor's psychic. Camille is right," he continued. "It's not what's on the outside that's so disgusting with people like yourself, but how UGLY you are inside that sickens people like us!"

"Well, she wanted it!" Carlton contested sharply. "You know, she's been prancing around all evening with that SEXY, TIGHT, LITTLE—"

James then landed his first blow on the agent's face. A flurry of punches followed. James punched Carlton's sides, his gut, then back and around to his face, relentlessly releasing his anger.

"Why, you dirty SON OF A BITCH!" he blasted.

Minutes later, Carlton had two broken ribs, a bloodied mouth with three missing teeth, and a fractured jaw as he bewailed in agony, then passed out.

JAMES AND CAMILLE

Monte Carlo: 1999

21

Several hours later, slowly flipping his eyes open, Carlton awoke to a dark and fuzzy dungeon. A throbbing headache was killing him as he was lying on top of an operating table. Gagged and strapped in a straight-jacket with adjustable buckles, his mouth was dry. Camille and James were nowhere in sight.

Carlton's eyes darted around, and a bizarre feeling came over him. A vintage railroad lantern sat on the table close by, fiercely blinding him. Highly discombobulated, he had lost all sense of direction from being all drugged up. He felt as if he was floating in space, split six different ways. And that his brain had shrunk down to a matchbox. It was the most outré position he had ever experienced.

He attempted to clear his vision. The dungeon was a makeshift operating room from the Dark Ages, with a collection of medieval surgical tools, exotic weaponry, and armor for war battles. The setting reminded him of a good murder-mystery thriller—except that he was the victim.

Objects were hung on the walls or showcased inside glass cabinets with appropriate lighting as if in a famous museum. Flashes of a vintage camera snapped on all sides while low-volume classical music played in the background as the minutes ticked by. Moments after what felt like an eternity, a figure wearing distinct stiletto heels slowly approached him, grabbing the lantern on the way. The lights came back on. A hazy figure stood in front of him, but his vision quickly sharpened.

Once again, the audacious and enigmatic Camille Rogers came into clear view—absolutely stunning. Poised in her usual glamorous persona, puffing a cigarette, she was "back to business," more confident than ever.

"Wake up, sleepy head," greeted the heiress in a sultry voice. "Virginia Woolf has caught up with you." She then blew heavy smoke at his face while stripping the tape off his mouth.

Carlton instantly felt the pain. "What is going on here? Where am I?" he coughed, looking around.

Camille looked hideously diabolical with a malevolent look of satisfaction on her face. "A not so pleasant place for you to find yourself, Agent Carlton," she replied with a deadpan voice. "I personally call it HELL."

Emerging from the shadows, James slowly appeared beside her. A pervasive shadow of darkness loomed over the vulnerable agent as the two gazed— looking very committed. Terror permeated the air; the scene became eerily thick and dark. Carlton could only imagine what would happen to him next.

"You shouldn't have come, Agent Carlton," said James impassively.

"Tsk-tsk. What a shame," Camille echoed his sentiments.

"I can't promise I'll be able to save you now," James continued.

"Sshhh! Don't spoil the surprise for him, darling!" warned Camille. "Since today is HIS lucky day," she added, then faced the agent. "You, my friend, get to be my LUCKY WINNER."

Carlton's heart pounded. "Wait! Stop! I'm sorry!" He implored nervously. "I seem to have lost track of time. I really don't know what happened. I'm really confused, you know," he smiled faintly.

Camille stole a glance at James, then turned back to the agent.

"Well then, let's get you unconfused, SWEET—HEART." She said dryly, winking back at him. Smiling at James, she asked. "Shall we get to work, my darling?"

"Indeed!" he agreed willingly.

Camille took off her expensive fur and jewels. Laying them on a chair, she slipped on a white laboratory jacket and put on surgical gloves. So did James.

"Let's start by—" she began. "Hand me the scalpel, James. I don't want to be sloppy tonight," she cautioned. "This one is quite special, don't you agree?"

"I sure do, mon chéri," he smiled.

James carried out Camille's wishes. He gingerly opened up a packet of vintage surgical tools and knives, laying each on a silver tray. An operation was now in progress. Handing over a few white towels, he gave her a scalpel, scissors, and a mini hatchet next. Horrified beyond words as he watched the two prepare, Carlton's eyes almost flew out of their sockets.

"What are you doing?" he swallowed nervously.

"I tell you what we're going to do, Agent Carlton," Camille remarked. "A little nipping and tucking will do."

"Stick a couple of needles in your brain for you to think better," overlapped James.

"Make an incision to your vital organ so we can properly diagnose your black liver," she continued.

"My liver?" Carlton interrupted, trying to keep up.

"That's right!" Camille stressed. "You've been slamming that Jack Daniels forever. There aren't enough bars in this town to serve slobs like you!" Looking him straight in the eyes, she softened her tone. "In other words, Agent Carlton, we just want to make you a BETTER man. But don't you worry—we've had plenty of practice before," she smiled deviously.

Suddenly, Camille noticed the hammer hatchet she was holding.

"Um, excuse me, darling?" she questioned. "What in God's green earth is this?" She tossed it back to James."

James was muddled.

"A scalpel," he replied. "You said scalpel, right?"

"Help me out here—" Camille continued calmly. "But are you trying to be a moron, or is that your actual state?" she derided.

"Look! I know what a scalpel is, OK?" James replied sharply. "So don't treat me like I don't know what I'm doing! I taught you how to use everything, for God's sake!"

"Yeah?" She jeered back.

Irritated, Camille erupted in a temper tantrum. Taking a few tools from the table, she walked toward James and slammed them on top of the agent's chest as if it was a concrete table.

"Here!" she said angrily.

"OW!" Carlton screamed.

"This is what we call a scalpel!" Camille explained, holding up a scalpel. "Not this!" She held up a different instrument. "Or this!" She held up another. "Or this!" And another. "Not even this! Got it? Now, how hard can that be!" she disparaged him.

James was utterly embarrassed. Tired of her constant carping and making him look like the world's greatest failure, he tossed back the hammer hatchet, hitting Carlton in the head as though he didn't even exist. "What-the-F—!" Carlton reacted, his face grimacing.

"What're you whining about?" James retaliated. His body was tensed with fury. "That's a scalpel! You asked for a scalpel, and I gave you one!"

"You GAVE me one?" Camille responded haughtily. "What does that even mean?"

The powerless agent was on pins and needles. His eyes followed every sharp object being thrown.

"Camille, I'm warning you!" James yelled out.

"Well, I stand warned!" retaliated Camille.

James was in his final straw.

"That's it! I give up!" he blurted. "I'm out of here!"

He began to walk away.

"All right! All right!" Camille halted. "Don't be so overdramatic, for God's sake! Everyone is so touchy around here," she said. "I guess I'm stuck with Dr. Moron here—you know what I mean, Agent Carlton?" she winked at him. "Now, pardon the interruption, but I believe a fruitful discussion was underway?"

"Yeah, I was saying to let me go," Carlton reiterated nervously. "And that uh...we can just forget about the whole thing?" he added.

Camille ruminated for a moment as if willing to let him go. "So, forget about the whole thing, huh?" she nodded in agreement, pursing her lips.

Carlton saw a glimpse of hope.

"Yeah, that's right," he encouraged. "I won't even mention this to the Monaco police," he continued. "Or the FBI. I thought if—"

"Well, I can't, you PIG!" she screamed.

Camille threw a wild outburst, raging violently. She stabbed Carlton through his carotid artery only an inch from his heart with a twelve-inch dagger.

"AAAAHHH! Son-of-a-bitch!" Carlton cried out.

Camille then gathered herself as she prepared for the procedure.

"James, get my antiseptic and scalpel, please," she instructed him flatly.

"Coming, mon chéri!" he complied.

Cutting several inches to the side of Carlton's straightjacket, Camille rubbed Povidone Iodine on the upper right part of his stomach, preparing his skin for an incision.

"I have an idea, Agent Carlton," she said. "Why don't we play a fun game rather than boring ones you sexual deviants LOVE so much? Now—which organs would you like me to take out first? Your lungs? Spleen? Liver anyone?" she asked.

"You don't have to do this!" Carlton pleaded. "Please! I won't say anything! I promise!"

Terrified beyond belief, he closed his eyes, hoping to avoid injury. But Camille continued to poke her fingers around his body in search of the perfect organ.

"That's cute, Agent Carlton," she replied. "It's always nice to hear agents BEG for a change," she noted. "But I think I'll settle for your liver instead." Then she swiftly took a stab at the agent's stomach with a scalpel.

"AAAHHH! You're CRAZY!" Carlton screamed in agony.

"So, I've been told," Camille responded dryly.

James thoroughly enjoyed watching the agent wince in pain. If there was ever a time the two felt vindicated for what they had suffered during childhood—this was it. As for the hapless agent, his nightmare had only just begun.

* * *

Hours passed. The chilly break of dawn welcomed the most diabolical scene. Trapped inside a wicked torture chamber guaranteeing pure pain and suffering, Carlton was tormented slowly and methodically beyond what he could fathom.

Camille faithfully enacted her darkest deed. She took out a glass vial, held it upward, punctured the rubber cap with a syringe needle, and injected it back into the agent. Carlton passed out for the second time.

She then proceeded to make a small incision in his stomach with medical precision. Blood slowly dripped down, creating a small pool underneath Carlton's body and smearing her white laboratory jacket. James silently filmed the process on camera.

Slipping in her middle and index fingers, Camille tried to feel Carlton's liver. She snipped a piece of tissue with a pair of scissors and placed it in a glass jar filled with ethanol liquid.

She looked straight into the camera and began to explain herself effortlessly as though she were some world-renowned medical expert in the middle of a procedure, giving a lecture to a group of wide-eyed interns.

"And "Viola!" she said aloud. "That, ladies and gentlemen, is how it's done." She held up another tissue sample with the scissors for everyone to see. "Easy does it, just like picking up your local escargot," she smiled.

"And CUT!" said James as he placed down his camera. "I guess that should wrap it up for now."

Minutes later, Camille dissolved a white-powder substance into a liquid and filled up the syringe again. She injected yet another drug into Carlton to counteract the drugs in his system, but not potent enough to kill him just yet.

James began to shave the top part of Carlton's hairline while Camille drilled a hole into his skull. Then ever so carefully, she stuck a ten-inch needle into the agent's brains and scraped away the connective tissue in the anterior part of his frontal lobes. Like a surgeon operating in the late 1800s, she too was required to perform in front of a live audience—as the "lobotomizing" of her patient was underway.

"And that should do it!" she glanced back at the camera. "By performing this neurosurgical procedure otherwise known as leukotomy, we have now removed the frontal lobe of his brain, repositioning how his brain works. It will give the patient a much calmer personality. Consequently, Agent Carlton is now a changed man," she continued proudly. "Free of any delusions, obsessions, and most notably, Mesdames et Messieurs—his male prowess as a sexual predator."

Camille had systematically broken the impudent agent down, piece by piece.

Even though James appeared to be the architect of all murders, it was Camille who remained the mastermind.

Finally, the elusive killer Carlton had been hunting down was unveiled. Like a chameleon, Camille had many faces. She was behind all the gruesome killings, including Jane Doe in Côte d'Azur, John Doe in Beverly Hills, and her "alter ego" Dr. K, who set death traps for those who entered her lair not imagining for a second that they would never leave. Her teen victims would be so much better off—she had actually saved them—or so she believed in her own twisted mind. Camille sought love for killings.

The Chateau had a labyrinth of passage hallways intended to disorient anyone from trying to escape, including a walk-in steel vault where victims were rendered unconscious—left to suffocate and die—and a secret gas chamber disguised as a nondescript room piping in poisoned gas through the vents. Dark side walls muffled their screams.

Bodies were disposed of in a pit made of lime, thereby melting their bones. James would incinerate them in high-heat furnaces, ridding all remaining evidence. This precision operation had managed to escape detection for years. A cold-blooded psychopath, Camille was a bloodthirsty killer bent on avenging every pain she and James suffered during their childhood and beyond.

Moments later, Carlton, incredibly sluggish, heard distant laughter. He glimpsed a murky image of Camille chatting away with James in a distant corner, both sipping their afternoon tea. Certain of his fate, Carlton knew it was only a matter of time before he would die. Suddenly, he felt a faulty buckle loosen up from his straightjacket. He managed to free up one arm, discreetly reaching down to feel his extra gun strapped below his knee. Camille saw movement and headed over.

"Having fun yet, Agent Carlton?" she smiled wickedly.

Grumbling under his breath, Carlton topped it off with a laugh. James proceeded according to plan, pulling out an antique bow saw and axe, a set of large knives, and old-fashioned hammers as though the final round of dismemberment had arrived.

"Oh, come on, Agent Carlton," James added. "You surely can do better than that?"

"You two are never going to get away with this," Carlton muttered as blood spilled out the sides of his mouth. "I've told the Monaco police to look for me if I'm not back at a certain time, which means—" he shouted. "YOU TWO ARE ALREADY DEAD!" He then laughed deliriously, choking on his own blood.

"I beg your pardon, monsieur?" Camille countered sharply.

"He's a babbling fool, that's all!" James replied.

Calming her voice, Camille asked, "Tell me, Agent Carlton, is that all Bureau swine like you ever do? I do wonder if they have grown tired of having you in their picnics and groundhog days," she mocked, turning around and walking away.

Mustering his last strength, Carlton quickly pulled out his gun. From his vantage point, he targeted a clear shot at Camille's back. James' heart skipped a beat. His eyes widened as Carlton cocked his gun, getting ready to fire. In his most daring move, James heroically jumped in front of Camille as shots rang out.

"NOOOO!" James screamed.

The bullet instantly hit James in the stomach. His knees buckled. Carlton dropped the gun and fell to the ground. Enraged, Camille picked up the gun and fired back at the agent, emptying the last of his bullets. BANG. BANG. BANG. BANG. BANG. Carlton died within seconds. She then rushed over to James and leaned him up against the wall. Camille was totally crushed.

"OH MY GOD! James, WHY?" she wept. "Why did you do it? I would have taken the bullet for you—you know that!"

"Because that pig was going to kill you," he gasped for air. "I had to do something, mon chéri."

The two laughed together for the last time. As their laughter faded, tenderness flashed across Camille's face. She looked into his eyes and said, "I can't lose you, James." Then Camille gently kissed him on the lips.

It was the moment James had been waiting for his entire life. Camille felt something for him. That he was more than just her best friend, and above all—she loved him back. James kissed her back, but started to lose his breath.

"Don't you dare die on me, James!" a distraught Camille shouted. "I'll take you to the hospital now!"

Seconds later, muffled sounds of sirens echoed from miles away. Camille stuck her neck out to the nearest window, then gave James a knowing look.

"It's the police," she surmised. "We better get out of here and get you to the Princess Grace Hospital."

But James grew weaker.

"No, no hospital. Plea..." he insisted in a breathy voice.

"It's not for you to decide!" Camille replied sharply. "I'm taking you there whether you like it or not!"

Camille first tried to prevent James from bleeding further. Looking around, she found white towels and wrapped them around his badly wounded stomach.

"Here." She took his hand and placed it on top of his stomach to hold the towel. "You must keep applying pressure until we get there," she instructed firmly.

Camille took his arm and placed it over her shoulder. Hobbling their way to the elevator, they reached the subterranean garage. She helped James settle into the passenger's seat of her blue Bugatti Eb110, then came around to the other side to start the car. Backing up in reverse, she swiftly pulled out of the garage, screeching her tires. Her mind raced frantically as she waited for the gates to open.

"Come on, come on," she whispered. "Oh, COME ON!" she repeated loudly. Turning to James, she said, "Hang on, James! Hang in there for me!"

Camille flew through her massive gates. With a ferocious grip on the wheel, she barreled down, gunning for the fastest road, searching for every alternative route and shortcut she could think of, desperately trying to rescue James.

"It's not going to be long, James!" she assured. "We're almost there! HANG ON!"

But James was becoming increasingly pale, slipping in and out of consciousness. Despite applying pressure on his wound with a blood-soaked towel, blood dripped between his fingers.

Camille was now hearing the groans of a dying man.

CAMILLE

Monte Carlo: 1999

22

Camille arrived at the prestigious Princess Grace Hospital Center and pulled up to the main entrance. Jumping out of the car, she screamed desperately for help while onlookers from a side street gawked in silence. "Se il vous plait! Aidez-moi!"

A newly-hired female employee in light pink scrubs rushed over to assist the panicked heiress. She determined quickly that James' gunshot wound could be fatal and that he was in dire need of medical attention.

"Nous avons ici une situation d'urgence!" the very alarmed employee called out for back-up. "Nous avons besoin d'une sauvegarde— MAINTENANT!"

A team of medical staff rushed out from behind the sliding doors, assisting in every way they could. Seconds later, James was on a gurney being carried into the emergency room with Camille tightly holding his hand. Camille and the frenzied team rushed through the posh hallways.

"I really...I'm not going to make it," James gasped.

"Don't talk like that, James!" Camille replied sharply, wiping her tears with her other hand. "You'll make it! Do you hear me? Just hang in there for me, please!"

Camille knew that she had to be strong for James. She needed to behave confidently as if his very life depended on her. But she could not help but think what might become of him as he laid there in peril. If he didn't make it, she would be left all alone. Her stomach could not churn any faster. She tried to enter the emergency room. The same accommodating employee who helped her outside suddenly blocked her from entering.

"Are you a family member, madame?" asked the French woman in a stern voice.

"Oh, Christ!" Camille snapped. "What is it with this Mrs. thing!" She then gathered herself and continued calmly. "It's Miss. And the answer is yes. I mean, no, but I am! But—what's the difference?" she shouted.

"Well! Mademoiselle!" the snooty employee huffed. "We only follow the rules here!"

Camille was furious. "Who is this CLOWN?" she muttered under her breath, looking around. "And WHAT is your name?" she said, pulling a cigarette from her purse. "And WHERE is your Hospital Director?"

"I'm sorry, but you cannot smoke here, mlle" the employee lectured. "And your threats won't be necessary. But if you refuse to give me an answer, I must ask you to leave the property right now."

"MON DIEU! Tu te tais jamais?" Camille said aloud, amazed at the woman's blathering.

"Mademoiselle! I'm sorry, but if you continue to behave like this, then I'm afraid I'm going to have to call security," the woman persisted.

Camille's voice grew powerful. "LADY! DO YOU EVEN KNOW WHO I AM?" she replied haughtily.

"No, mademoiselle."

"For your information—I AM CAMILLE ROGERS," revealed the frustrated heiress. "And if you don't straighten this out right now, I will make sure you clean toilets for the rest of your French life—GOT IT? Now darling, do you really want to see your mouth stitched up to your nose?" Hmm?"

Perplexed by this bizarre response, the employee stood utterly speechless. It was hard enough to deal with patients on the mental ward. When guests refused to adhere to the hospital's policies, it made her life even more difficult.

But time was simply running out for Camille to be by James' side. Not even a self-important worker would prevent her from doing just that. Camille refused to be told what to do her entire professional life. She was the one who gave orders. And if this employee knew who she was, much less than her net worth and the conglomerate of companies she owned, the tide would certainly turn. Not to mention that her mother, Claire Rogers, was one of the founding members of the hospital. Claire and Camille had donated millions of Euros since its opening day in 1977.

More significantly, the employee would not have dared to address her this way if she were aware that Camille was a huge benefactor of the hospital and her close relationship with the Prince—a member of the Board of Directors. By contrast, she would be kissing the ground Camille walked on and would go out of her way to please her. Given the encumbrances, nobody in their right mind would tell Camille what to do. Nobody.

"No, mademoiselle," the bewildered employee replied. "Of course not."

"Well then—LET ME THROUGH!" demanded Camille. "Look, he's about to die in there, and I'm not going to let that happen! That's it! I'm going in!"

Camille tried to walk past her. To her amazement, the stubborn lady prevented her from entering yet again.

"I'm terribly sorry mlle, but you really can't go in there!" she insisted. "You must wait for security!"

"THE HELL I WILL! Allez vous faire foutre!" exclaimed the heiress. She pushed the nuisance employee aside. The woman was shaken as she fell down on the floor, hitting her head on the wall.

Camille then burst into the emergency room. She immediately saw James lying unconscious on top of the operating table as pandemonium broke out.

"Mlle, you shouldn't be here," a nurse warned softly.

"C'est bon, c'est Mlle Rogers," a doctor told the nurse to let her through, to bypass the hospital's protocol.

"Merci," Camille said breathlessly as she quietly settled on a chair. But her heart instantly dropped. She could neither feel her feet touch the floor nor hear herself breathe. A team of first-class doctors and registered nurses raced to plug all sorts of drain and suction tubes into James' mouth and stomach, using surgical tools as they tried to stabilize his condition.

He was hooked up to an IV and electrocardiogram machine that monitored his heart rate and blood pressure, fighting for his life. Camille stopped dead in her tracks as the thought of him dying entered her mind. After her mother's death, Camille renounced her faith in the Catholic religion and never once looked back. Convinced that she had been deserted as a child when she suffered violent beatings by her adopted mother, the childhood innocence stolen by her father irreparably damaged her for life.

From the outset, believing her life was cursed, Camille had become quite a cynic. She developed the worst kind of paranoia—harboring hatred, fury, and total distrust for the motives of those she met.

With poor coping mechanisms, Camille was blinded to anything good life had to offer, except for James. She confronted her personal demons by avoiding the outside world as much as possible, becoming a bitter recluse succeeding at every level.

By and large, living under the care of James meant one thing—SHE WOULD NEVER GET HURT AGAIN. Camille slowly turned away from the light and was gradually swept into the darkness.

But even at this critical juncture, she reconnected with God in the purest way. Unlike her sanctimonious mother, a religious zealot pretending to be a pious devotee, Camille disdained such behaviors all her life. Desperately seeking God's comfort and guidance, she humbled herself. Tears streamed down her face as she reflected. In this moment of truth, she bared her soul in the most unadulterated fashion for the first time.

"I know I have strayed away from you in the past," she prayed. "But if you give me this one chance... PLEASE, God, don't let him die... I love him."

Minutes later, James went into cardiac arrest. Doctors screamed "code blue" as they tried to resuscitate him. Collectively, they exhausted every available medical option. Still, it was a futile effort.

It was as if God was finally demanding payment for her sins. Camille's faith was being tested in some kind of divine intervention. Fearing the worst, she struggled to breathe. Her eyes darted from James to his heart machine, then to his body as she paced back and forth, praying for a miracle.

Suddenly, James flatlined, and Camille went into a state of panic. Rushing forward, screaming in a deafening tone, she landed in the arms of two nurses who restrained her. Continuing their battle to save James, the team could not bring him back. A deadly silence followed.

In the stillness of the moment, not a sound broke but the thumping beat of Camille's broken heart. Unable to accept her fate with James, it felt as though the great life she once lived was about to swing in the other direction. But things were about to get a lot worse. Much worse.

Like a giant oscillating pendulum suddenly changing course, Camille was on a journey back to her painful past—riddled with pain and sorrow. The wealth and power bestowed upon her were meaningless. She had utterly failed to control or alter the trajectory of her life.

Reeling back, she experienced numbness throughout her chest and body. Transformed into a frightened five-year-old girl, she slid down the sidewall, sobbing like a lost child, totally helpless—abandoned for good. Camille was now experiencing the unspeakable pain so unfamiliar to her usual afflictions that there was no help or hope in sight. Realizing the enormity of her loss, she gasped for air.

In spite of their differences, James was close to perfection. She had never met anyone quite like him—and would be hard-pressed to find someone even close. James was the light of her life, her dream companion, her idyllic friend who never once gave up on her—despite her difficult and often glaring flaws. He saw the good in her even when no one else could and her potential for becoming a better person, one who could give great love if only she opened up her heart.

He understood her past. He had the purest and kindest regard for Camille written in his heart—as though he was born to look after her. He was her white knight in shining armor who never failed to rescue her in incalculable ways.

The two shared indelible memories of love, pain, happiness, and devotion to one another. They were soul mates for eternity from the day they met. Bonded for life, Camille and James were kindred spirits. They were deeply connected better than any couple on earth. They broke barriers, transcended time, and achieved more together than anyone expected—and they did it all without a single regret. Losing James, the impossibility of accepting his absence, would be her undoing. Totally reliant on his ability to care for her, she would never find her way back.

All the days they shared that seemed so long now seemed short— relegated to a collection of memories. Camille had yet to learn how to live life without him. Whatever she and James were meant to do here on earth had been reduced to just one fleeting moment. Reflecting in sadness, she now appreciated life as if the incoming days were her last. Everything in this world, including her life, was suddenly temporal. The ephemeral joys of her childhood with James at the French Riviera had vanished.

She then thought about the dying children she visited in hospitals around the world: lonely orphans who craved loving homes; undernourished youngsters with bodies ravaged by disease and illness, awaiting a miracle; and disadvantaged children born with disabilities.

Camille mused about the joys of birthing a new life and the sorrow that accompanies death. And lastly, she thought about abused children who long to be saved from the evils tormenting their souls daily. The pain she endured as a child suddenly seemed so irrelevant.

On a day like this, she could see only one path ahead. Her entire being, her sensibility, and her self-worth were pushing her in a new direction. As if her life story was being played out beautifully like scenes in a movie.

Looking out of the glass window, Camille saw beautiful clouds slowly floating by ever so peacefully against the bluest sky. She ached to be with James in the afterlife. Overwhelmed by profound sadness and loneliness, she yearned for his presence. The obvious line of demarcation between the ground she stood on, and the transcendental heaven of God now seemed indistinguishable. Heaven was far closer than anyone would have imagined.

Losing her best friend created a wound that would never heal. He would linger like a phantom limb throughout her body forever. And just like that, James faded away. His lifeless body—once full of vigor and strength—lay immobile, cooling down rapidly to room temperature as Camille saw it. His beautiful blue eyes would witness no more pain and suffering. Camille, bereft of all happiness, finally lost the one and only person who truly mattered. Neither riches nor glittering diamonds could resurrect him.

The woman of glitz and glamour, who saved children across three continents, could not save the person she loved the most. Grief-stricken, staring into space, Camille was unable to move. Never again would they dream together. Never again would they have glorious times to treasure. Never again would they laugh forever. All that was good seemed forever shrouded by darkness. Camille was completely and utterly heartbroken.

THE END

CPSIA information can be obtained
at www.ICGtesting.com
Printed in the USA
BVHW042318290922
PP14087800001B/1

9 781945 674396